To Danny on his birthday!.

Anthony; family

The Secret Life of Billie's Uncle Myron

LEN JENKIN AND EMILY JENKINS

The Secret Life
of Billie's Uncle Myron

HENRY HOLT AND COMPANY · NEW YORK

Henry Holt and Company, Inc.
Publishers since 1866
115 West 18th Street
New York, New York 10011

Henry Holt is a registered
trademark of Henry Holt and Company, Inc.

Published in Canada by Fitzhenry & Whiteside Ltd.,
195 Allstate Parkway, Markham, Ontario L3R 4T8.

Library of Congress Cataloging-in-Publication Data
Jenkin, Len. The secret life of Billie's Uncle Myron/
by Len Jenkin and Emily Jenkins.
   p.   cm.
Summary: Because her rock star parents fail to give her
enough attention, eleven-year-old Billie stows away in
Uncle Myron's Cadillac and joins him in fantastic travels.
[1. Runaways—Fiction.   2. Uncles—Fiction.   3. Fantasy.]
I. Jenkins, Emily.   II. Title.
PZ7.J4115Se   1996   [Fic]—dc20   96–3820

ISBN 0-8050-4395-0
First Edition—1996

Printed in the United States of America
on acid-free paper. ∞

10   9   8   7   6   5   4   3   2   1

For our moms,
JOHANNA JENKINS *and* BEATRICE JENKIN

Contents

Rock Tour

Billie aimed carefully. She flicked a juicy spitball right onto the back of the Pigbone's neck. Her marksmanship was perfect. She could see the spit oozing down into her tutor's collar as he droned on. And on. And on.

"Tallahassee is the capital of Mississippi," he said in that low breathy voice of his. "Sacramento is the capital of Massachusetts. New Jersey, of course, is the capital of California. Kansas City, you'll be interested to know, is not the capital of Kansas."

"You fascinate me," Billie assured the Pigbone.

"Instead, Billie, my dear, it's the capital of Minneapolis."

"I'm not your dear Billie."

The tutor smiled weakly and pointed in the general direction of Kansas City on the large map he had attached to the wall of their hotel room. They were in the Princess Suite. Billie flicked another spitball. Bull's-eye!

"The great state of Minneapolis," continued the Pigbone, "is noted for its endless highways without bathrooms and for its large cities without playgrounds. We go there next week, I believe."

He's ignoring those spitballs, Billie thought, just to drive me crazy. Her two-year-old brother, Bix, was rolling around and around on the king-size hotel bed, about to pop from giggling so hard. He was just learning to make spitballs himself.

Billie and Bix were united in the torture of their tutor, Llewellyn Pigbone. His real name was something else, of course. Billie had forgotten it by now. Pigbone was better for him, anyway. He was short and round and had a weak English way of talking. He was probably the most boring man alive. Billie knew very well where Kansas City actually was. She'd been there four times already with her parents.

She had also been to Rome, Paris, London, and Las Vegas, because her parents were almost always on tour. They had been jetting around the world for over a year this time, touching down occasionally at their penthouse in New York City. Billie's mother, Mimi, was incredibly famous. She did ads for Diet Coke and her face had made the covers of *Interview*, *Spin*, and *Rolling*

Stone. She had even hosted *Saturday Night Live.* Billie had stayed up to watch it.

Together, Mimi and Billie's father, Brian, were the rock group Euphoria. Their latest single, "Neon Sky," was number one on the charts. Brian and Mimi played every night to sold-out crowds across the country. Then they had to sign autographs and celebrate and meet executives and old friends from whatever city they were in and celebrate some more and then wind down and fall into bed at the break of dawn. That's why they were still asleep in the master bedroom of the Princess Suite, even though it was three in the afternoon.

"So much for geography," said the Pigbone. The USA disappeared with a flip of his pudgy wrist, and he pulled another chart down from the roll-up on the wall. This one was covered with French verbs. *"Bienvenue à la France,"* he announced.

Billie got up from the table and went over to the window. They were on the top floor. She looked out over skyscrapers, freeways, huge advertising billboards. What city was she in?

She had no idea.

Behind her, the Pigbone was telling a story in French about two dumb kids who lived in Paris. *"Bonjour, Yvette. Aimez-vous la Tour Eiffel?"* he minced. Billie had been there five times. The Pigbone paused in his recitation. Before he could say, "Are you listening, Billie dear?" Billie reassured him.

"I'm memorizing every word. *Continue, s'il vous plaît*." Once she and Bix had locked themselves in the bathroom for two hours to escape a French lesson. *"Non! Non! Non!"* they had chanted from behind the closed door. Luckily, they had been staying at the Ritz in Dallas that week, where there were perfume samples in the bathroom. Billie had tried all of them and decorated Bix's face with her mother's lipstick before they fell asleep on the bath mat.

Finally the Pigbone stopped blabbing and gave her a break while he sorted through his stacks of papers. Billie ran to the telephone. "Room service, please." The lecture had made her hungry, and she had befriended the headwaiter the night before.

"Omaha Splendide Café."

"Hello, Mr. Eggwater? It's Billie. I need an order of barbecue ribs. Desperately. And Bix is flopping off the bed. He needs nourishment. He's wasting away! The suffering in the Princess Suite is worse than you can imagine! Save the Children!"

"Three vanilla puddings, as usual?" asked Mr. Eggwater. He remembered Bix's regular order. The sign of a true professional.

"Yes," answered Billie. "Pudding's all he'll eat. Also,

two breakfast specials, double bacon. Thanks." Just in case Brian and Mimi woke up, she wanted to have breakfast waiting for them.

One evening last week, in some other city, she and Bix had eaten dinner while their parents ate breakfast. They'd all gone downstairs to the hotel restaurant at six P.M. The whole meal had been totally embarrassing. Brian had worn leather pants and his pajama top. Even in the dark dining room, Mimi wore sunglasses so people wouldn't recognize her. She brought three jars of vitamin powder down with her and mixed spoonfuls into her orange juice. Her personal trainer, a bodybuilder named Roberta, had her on some special diet for more energy and muscle definition. Brian ate breakfast *and* dessert, putting peppermint ice cream on his scrambled eggs. Billie stirred her spaghetti around on the plate and looked enviously at the family at the next table. They were tourists, two girls and their parents. They wore bright-colored shirts and had sunburns across their noses. They had just come back from the aquarium. She could tell because the older girl was wearing a hat with a killer whale on it and the younger one had a balloon. They were all eating dinner like normal people. The dad wore a sport jacket and ordered a steak, like dads are supposed to.

After that night, Billie decided to stick with room

service. Eating out with Brian and Mimi just reminded her how different her life was from other kids'.

Billie lay back on the bed and looked up at the ceiling. If only the Pigbone would teach me something interesting—something worth knowing, she thought. If only there was somebody on tour to talk to besides maids and headwaiters. She did have Bix, but he wasn't much company. Most of the time he was just annoying, always playing with his horrible Cosmodemon action figures. He was scared to play with other kids in the hotel swimming pools, but he had a stupid friendship with each ugly plastic creature. In fact, they were his only friends. He even spoke to them in his own secret language. "Gorpus mogore bluto," he would say to something hiding in his pocket as they waited for room service to bring the pudding. "Floopus blixin filco," he'd say as he chased his father around the room, holding a figure that looked like G.I. Joe with the head of a tyrannosaurus. Lately he'd been talking to Billie in this secret language, too. That morning he'd woken her up with a hearty "Klaatu barada nikto."

Billie was a little worried about him. Shouldn't he be talking normally by now? Mimi thought he was cute. "He's just a little behind," she'd say, "but he's going to catch up soon and astound everyone with his genius. He'll be a wonderboy! Won't you, Bixie baby?"

"Foofus," Bix would gurgle. Needless to say, French was not his strong point.

Over in a corner, the Pigbone was fidgeting nervously with his glasses. "Billie," he pleaded, "we must return to our *leçon*." He looked as if he was about to cry. Billie almost felt sorry for him. She was about to ask him to please tell her more about Yvette's feelings for the Eiffel Tower when she heard a loud *OOOGA! OOOGA!* coming from the street. Billie knew that sound. Not many noises reached all the way to the fifty-ninth floor. She and Bix flew to the window and leaned out. Billie grabbed the back of her brother's T-shirt to stop him from tumbling down into the street and splattering himself across the pavement.

Sure enough, swinging gracefully into a parking space right in front of a fire hydrant was a sky-blue 1958 Cadillac convertible. It had enormous tailfins and a real foghorn bolted to the front hood. Uncle Myron was here. He *OOOGA-OOOGA*ed the foghorn again, confusing all the traffic nearby, and Billie could see the shiny top of his bald head in the driver's seat.

"He's here, isn't he?" A tall, stylish figure leaned in the doorway to the master bedroom. It was Mimi, looking rumpled but glamorous in a green silk kimono given her by some love-struck record producer.

"Yes!" cried Billie, running to give her a hello kiss.

"Mixolt!" squealed Bix, and jumped down from the windowsill. Mimi rumpled Bix's hair and scooped him up. Billie grabbed on to her leg. Her mother's toenails were painted black with little silver stars on them.

"Ahem!" The Pigbone coughed loudly into his puffy hand.

"Howdy, Seymour," Mimi said, lighting a cigarette with a gold lighter. Billie wished she wouldn't smoke.

"The children are in a lesson," he whimpered.

"Even Bixie?" asked Mimi, bouncing him onto the giant bed.

Bix screamed, "Towel Eiffus!"

"Billie and I were working on her French. If we're going to bring her up to sixth-grade level, we really must have adequate study time."

"All right, Seymour. Billie honey, get to those *savoir faire*s and *je ne sais quoi*s. You'll see your Uncle Mysterious later." Mimi grabbed Bix by the hand. "Come on, baby. Let's go down the hall and wait for Myron!" The two of them ran off toward the elevators, Bix's Euphoria World Tour T-shirt almost dragging on the ground. Mimi's famous voice sailed into a welcome song.

Uncle Myron is there, he's got no hair!
He sails through the air in his underwear!

Billie sighed and sat back down in her chair. What good was it to be the child of famous rock stars, when you never even saw them and all you got to do was stare at the inside of hotel rooms with maps and grammar diagrams taped up to the walls? No friends, no playgrounds, no pets, no Little League baseball team. This was not the good life. This was no life at all.

"Are we ready?" The Pigbone sneered. *"Bonjour, mademoiselle. Comment allez-vous?"*

The last time Uncle Myron had appeared was over a year ago, on the snowy evening of Billie's tenth birthday. After the party, with chocolate cake and paper crowns and Bix smearing the ice cream on the hotel bedspread, Uncle Myron's Cadillac rolled out of the darkness. The huge foghorn sounded *OOOGA! OOOGA!* and they had all rushed down to the lobby and out into the fast-falling snow with their shoes off. Uncle Myron had the top down, and the snow was piled on the seat alongside him, and on his bald head as well. The car's tape player was playing Billie Holiday's "Billie's Blues" in honor of the birthday girl and her namesake. He stepped out of the car, shook the snow off the fur collar of his big coat, and handed Billie a present. It was a pair of sunglasses with a heavy silver frame. They rested elegantly on crimson velvet in a matching silver case. The case was polished brightly, and Billie's name was etched on it in flowing script.

"Billie," Uncle Myron had boomed, slapping her on the back. "This is a very special present indeed! An extraordinary present! A particularly amazing present! It comes with my prediction that you'll become a particularly amazing sort of person." Who knew what Uncle Myron was talking about? The glasses didn't seem that amazing to Billie. But she loved them anyway. They made her feel grown-up and sophisticated.

Uncle Myron then gave Bix, who was only a baby, a box of super-violent Cosmodemon figures. One was a plastic rat with four eyes and jaws of steel. Another had the body of a man and the tail of a hideous scaly sea serpent. A third was dressed for battle in old-fashioned knight's armor. When you opened the visor it looked out at you with the face of a wild boar. Bix loved them. Uncle Myron bowed, got back in his car, and drove away into the dark.

No one knew where Uncle Myron lived or what work he did. He wouldn't tell them. "I do very important work indeed," he'd say, and blow his nose loudly. Billie believed he didn't work at all, but just ran around the universe having fun, living in his Cadillac. And he could have, too. The car was that huge.

By now, everyone else was in the next room: Mimi and Bix and Brian and Uncle Myron, and probably a room service waiter bringing cookies and cake and champagne and Cokes. No one seemed to care that Billie wasn't there, or if they did, they'd forgotten in the excitement of the moment. She could hear Uncle Myron's booming laugh through the half-opened door.

"Too distracting," said the Pigbone, and slammed it shut. "Now for your history lesson. Christopher Columbus had a passionate love affair with the queen of Spain. Yet he was only a scholar, a poor man of learning, a tutor to the royal . . ."

Billie didn't care about Columbus and his love affairs. Why did the Pigbone always compare himself to famous explorers? Did he have some sort of sicko obsession? And he never let her go early. She'd probably miss Uncle Myron completely. He never stayed more than an hour or two. "Too many places to get to," Myron would say. Nobody would know what places he was talking about, and before her mom and dad could ask, off he'd go.

Billie wandered over to the window and looked down. The sky-blue Cadillac was still at the curb.

"Billie?" The whispery voice of the Pigbone from behind her made her jump. He closed his book with a solid snap. "Now is not the time for pointless reverie. Now is the time to review the preeminent explorers of the New World: Vasco da Gama, Ludwig van Beethoven, and Ponce de León. Tell me, please, who discovered what?"

Billie barely heard the Pigbone. She was busy having a moment of beautiful certainty, mostly because she was feeling neglected and unimportant, but also because of a mad desire to misbehave.

That shiny blue convertible was calling to her. She'd be a stowaway. It would drive her parents crazy. They deserved it, too. If Billie had to go on tour and miss Little League, and not have a bicycle, and not have any friends, and stay in all these hotels (some of which had perfectly lousy room service), all so her parents could be with her, they could at least find the time to do it.

Oh, they wanted to, all right, but somehow there was always another interview, another party, or another show. They never listened to her when she was right next to them. Maybe they'd hear her better from a few hundred miles away.

2

Fishtail Cadillac

"Mr. Pigbone, sir, can I go pee?" asked Billie in her sweetest voice.

"Quickly, my dear Billie," answered the Pigbone. He was pleased to be spoken to respectfully for a change. "Vasco da Gama awaits you."

Instead of going to the bathroom, Billie slipped through the suite's living room to her bedroom. Grabbing her pink plastic purse, she hurriedly packed—tangerine lip gloss, candy canes left over from Christmas six months ago, and a peanut butter and Marshmallow Fluff sandwich that was supposed to have been yesterday's lunch. She scooped up her shades, but the silver case for them was nowhere to be found. Better forget it, Billie thought. Bix was always messing with her stuff.

Slipping on the shades, her plastic purse over one arm, Billie tiptoed back through the living room toward the door of the suite. In her parents' room she could see a flash of Mimi's platinum crewcut, Brian still sleepy in his bathrobe, and Uncle Myron, his great mustache waggling up and down. She could make out a few scattered words in Uncle Myron's booming voice: "roller lunchmeat . . . baseball chain"—or was that brain?—"rhinoceros underwear"—or did he say underwater?

Billie made it to the elevator unseen. The doors opened. Standing inside was Bix.

"Floxon rodor," he said.

"Floxon rodor yourself, Bixiebutt." Billie pressed L. The doors closed, and they sped down toward the lobby. Billie looked at herself and Bix in the elevator mirror. His favorite Cosmodemon figure, a bright orange warrior well chewed about the head, peeped out of his shirt. Next to him Billie seemed grown-up, daring, almost wild.

The elevator stopped, and the doors slid open. "I'm only going to the cigarette machine for Mimi," said Billie. "Go back upstairs. Bye-bye, Bixie." Bix giggled. He whispered, "Gorpus floopus" to his orange Cosmodemon. The elevator doors closed, and Bix was gone. Luckily, the lobby was pretty empty. Billie walked casually through the shiny revolving door.

There it was. Uncle Myron's Cadillac. Up close it was enormous. The tail fins soared up like a rocket ship. The top was down, but a striped blanket was tossed carelessly across the backseat. Billie had one leg up and over the side when she turned to glance back at the hotel.

Someone was watching her. Someone about as tall as a trash can. Bix. He giggled and slipped back into the revolving door. The door began to spin faster and faster as Bix raced hysterically around. Oh, no, Billie thought. The little snitch'll point to where I'm hiding, and they'll catch me. They'll sit me down and I'll have to answer a lot of questions about my *feelings*. I might as well go back upstairs right now. Or *else* I could . . .

Before she even finished her thought, Billie was running toward the revolving door. She threw herself into one compartment and slowed it to a stop, braking with her sneakers. Bix flew out toward the elevator, but Billie was quicker. She grabbed him by the wrist. "Sorry, Bix," Billie said, "but we have a crisis here. I gotta play rough." Bix scrunched up his eyes and started to wail.

Billie switched tactics. "Bixie baby brother bunny! Let's play a little game!" She smiled at him until her face almost cracked. It worked. Bix forgot his tears and smiled back at her. His big sister was going to play with him. He was in heaven. "Glorpus mogore, Billixa!" he shouted as he was dragged outside toward the huge Caddy at the curb.

Billie hid herself and Bix on the floor of the backseat, pulling the blanket over them. "Stay very quiet, Bixie," she whispered. "We're playing hide-and-seek, and Mimi and Brian will try to find us." Bix was far too excited to be quiet. "Goopo plautus bongo!" he squealed. Billie quickly unzipped her purse, grabbed a candy cane, and slipped it into Bix's mouth. The old pacifier trick. Bix gurgled with delight. He loved candy almost as much as he loved pudding.

As Billie watched her little brother demolish the candy cane, she realized something. Bix was only two, and he got to see Mimi and Brian as little as she did. Poor kid. He must miss his mom and dad. She leaned over and whispered in Bix's ear. "It's okay you're along, Bixie-boy. Let the rock stars worry about both of us."

Billie heard the Cadillac's door open and slam shut. Uncle Myron must be behind the wheel. He slapped in a tape. Billie Holiday's throaty voice began singing something about love and a cheap carnation. Why did they name me after her? wondered Billie. Her music is so boring. . . . Then the *OOOGA! OOOGA!* of the foghorn blared, and the big V-8 engine roared. The Cadillac surged forward with a great shock of speed, pressing Billie and Bix against the floor. From under the blanket, over the music and the motor, Billie could hear Uncle Myron singing along.

Don't give me no carnations, baby.
I'm a roses kind of girl. . . .

sang Uncle Myron joyously as Billie felt the car turn sharply around a corner. Had they really tilted up on two wheels, or was it just her imagination?

A rose is a rose is a rose.
The way to this girl's heart is through her nose!

The car turned again, slowed, and then screeched to a halt. "How may I help you today?" said a mechanical-sounding voice.

"I'll have a triple burger deluxe and a Strawberry Fizz," Uncle Myron shouted.

"Sorry, sir. Strawberry Fizz is not on our menu."

"Oops! Wrong side of the desert," said Uncle Myron to himself.

"Side of fries, sir?" said the mechanical voice.

"Just the burger!" said Myron, shouting again. "Oh, and I need some marshmallows."

"We only have mini marshmallows, sir. The ones for cocoa."

"I'll take a case."

"We don't sell them separately."

"Really?" Myron sounded heartbroken. "They're a gift for someone special."

"They're not on the menu, sir."

"Then give me a hundred cups of cocoa with marshmallows. And leave out the cocoa."

"One hundred and three dollars and forty-five cents. Wait for pickup."

"She'll love it," laughed Myron to himself, and he began to hum another song.

Billie kept still under the blanket. She was hungry, but if she tried to unwrap her sandwich, Myron might hear the noise. She remembered the barbecue and pudding that was probably arriving in the Princess Suite right now.

Will anybody notice I'm not there to eat it? Billie wondered. Probably not yet. Probably not until right before showtime tonight. Or even worse, maybe not till tomorrow morning. Or maybe nobody'll notice I'm gone for years and years. Mimi and Brian'll be old and have gray hair, and they'll be toddling around with their canes and Mimi'll say, "Turn up your hearing aid, Brian. I remember something. Don't we have a daughter? Named Roger or Bob or something? Where is that girl?"

Billie felt like crying. She was all set for a good sniffle when Uncle Myron's order came. He put the big cardboard box on the front seat, stepped on the gas, and the Cadillac shot out of the drive-through like a bullet.

"Filbert shimsham," whispered Bix, poking her. He was still playing hide-and-seek, and wondering why nobody had come to look for them yet.

"We're going on a trip, Bixie," Billie whispered. "We're having an adventure." As the Caddy glided along, Billie ached to peek out and see where they were. But what if Uncle Myron saw her? Would he be a typical grown-up and rush to telephone Mimi and Brian? Or would he be understanding and take them for ice cream? A mountain of brownie fudge, with lots of whipped cream. No walnuts, please. Or maybe a pint of raspberry swirl . . .

As Billie imagined the mountains of ice cream Uncle Myron might buy them, the Cadillac began to tilt. Were they going up a hill? Further and further they tilted, until it seemed as if they must be driving up the steepest mountain in the world.

Mount Everest, Billie thought. My crazy Uncle Myron is trying to drive up Mount Everest! He's driven us to Tibet and he's going to sled the Cadillac down a glacier. We'll crash into an ice gorge and get eaten by the Abominable Snowman. Mimi and Brian will read about us in the *National Enquirer*!

Before Billie could dream up a rescue helicopter to haul the Caddy out of the ice gorge, the car leveled out, and the ride became as smooth as pudding. Billie could feel they were still moving, but heard almost no sound except the soft hum of the motor. From a great distance, she thought she could hear the cries of birds.

She looked down at Bix, but he was snoozing, clutching the candy cane with fat sticky fingers. She scratched his head gently in the way he always liked. "You know, Bix," Billie whispered, "you're a terrible pest. But I still kinda love you." She curled up next to him and softly sang a ballad, one of Mimi's songs: "Up into the night I go . . ."

In a moment, she, too, was asleep.

3

Cairo T. Crow

Billie woke with a start, realizing she missed the hum of the motor. The Cadillac had stopped moving. How long had they been parked? She had no idea. She crawled out from under the blanket. It was dark. Uncle Myron wasn't in the driver's seat. Where was he?

Bix was still sleeping, so she tucked him in on the floor in the back and let him stay where he was. Mustering her courage, Billie crept out of the car. She was on a sandy stretch of desert next to a ramshackle building. Above her loomed a gleaming plastic sign: a crescent moon face, all painted silver. The words below it read SILVER MOON MOTEL. The moon winked its plastic eye open and shut. Billie felt for a moment that it was looking down at her in a disapproving way, like some stern, sour-faced judge. "You're breaking your mother's heart," it seemed to say. "She's crying over you in a hotel in Omaha." Billie stuck her tongue out at the big silver face.

Light shone from one of the motel rooms, and through the parted curtains she could see an extremely large crow perched on top of the television set. He was one of the strangest sights she had ever seen. He was wearing a leather cap and his matted feathers stuck out at odd angles. As she watched, he hopped down onto the table next to the TV and kicked the screen energetically with his skinny claw. Billie moved a few steps closer and peered in the window.

"Last time I stay in this cheapo rathole! Nothing ever works!" screeched the crow. It had a voice like a gangster in an old movie, deep and raspy. Suddenly the crow flung his room door open. He was looking Billie right in the eye.

"Maid service?" he said. "Hey! Some human help in the Borderland. That's what I like to see. Listen! The TV's acting up. Just when the Creature Feature is on. Fix it."

"I'm not the maid."

"I need more towels." Before she knew it, Billie was dragged inside to listen to the crow complain about his bill. "More towels and more durable appliances! And for what I'm paying, the walls should be entirely flat!" He waved one shiny black wing at a fresh hole in the plaster, and hopped up and down on one yellow foot. Billie finally had to yell to get his attention.

"I AM NOT THE MAID!"

"Liar," muttered the crow, and laughed a scratchy, dark kind of laugh. He hopped over to the dresser and poured himself a drink out of a bottle labeled "Strawberry Fizz." He poked his beak down to the bottom of the glass and took a sip of the bright pink liquid.

"What do you mean, 'liar'?" asked Billie indignantly.

"If you're not the maid," the crow squawked, "prove it."

"Do I look like a maid to you?" she spat. "Am I wearing a uniform? Do I have a name tag? Am I carrying a feather duster?"

The crow shrank back. "Don't say feather duster!" he screeched.

"Feather duster," said Billie, louder than before.

"Smart-ass kid," the crow mumbled, taking another drink of Fizz.

"I don't have to prove anything to you," snapped Billie. "I happen to be looking for my Uncle Myron."

"Myron?" The crow looked interested. "Your uncle, you say?"

"Yes," said Billie. "That's his Cadillac outside, and I—"

"Not anymore," interrupted the crow. "Your Uncle Myron is a gambling man. He lost that mean machine to me, Cairo T. Crow, just tonight in a card game. Fair and square. I stuck him with the Old Maid." He cackled with glee.

"I don't care about any Old Maid!" said Billie. She felt almost ready to cry, and it took a great effort to stop herself. "Please listen to me. I don't work here. I'm lost. I need to find my Uncle Myron." The crow took another sip of his Fizz, and this time he eyed Billie with some sympathy.

"I know what it's like to be lost, kid," he said. "You want some Strawberry Fizz? It'll relax you."

"I'm not allowed to drink relaxing beverages," said Billie. "My dad won't let me."

"My dad flew the coop when I was just a chick," confessed Cairo, reaching out his wing for the bottle. "I had a traumatic childhood." As he reached, Billie could see a playing card carefully hidden away among his shiny black feathers. It was the Old Maid. The crow sat back and took a drink. Billie thought she'd better ask him some questions before he finished off all that Fizz. It seemed to have a strong effect on him.

"Just where are we?"

"At the edge of the Endless Desert, where the Borderland begins. The Silver Moon is the Borderland motel."

"Borderland? Between what and what?"

"Between where you come from and where you're going," replied Cairo with a raspy chuckle. "And that Cadillac knows the road. It knows by heart all the crazy mixed-up geography of the Borderland and all the other worlds it touches. Mommie Darling souped it up." Here the crow lowered his voice to a whisper, as if he was afraid someone else was listening. His beak was almost stuck into Billie's ear: "That car can go *between* the worlds. And it's MINE!"

Billie was becoming more and more worried about herself and Bix. She had no idea where they were, or how they were going to get home.

"You wanna play a round of Old Maid?" asked Cairo.

"No thanks," she answered, thinking of the card tucked away among his feathers. This bird had probably cheated Uncle Myron out of his Cadillac. "Where *is* my uncle?" she demanded. "It's late, and I need to find him so he can take me home. Brian and Mimi might be worried. Besides, my baby brother Bix is asleep in the car, and he'll get cranky without his pudding." Suddenly the crow was paying attention, and his red-rimmed beady eyes began to gleam.

"Baby brother Bix?" he rasped. "How old is the charming child?"

"Two," answered Billie.

"A good age."

"For what?" said Billie. "Drooling?"

"Two is not only good," mused the crow, "it's perfect. Young and stupid . . . mushy as a piece of Play-Doh." He hopped up onto the floor lamp and balanced precariously on the shade, his leather cap tilted over one eye. Billie wondered if that Strawberry Fizz would be legal in New York.

"It's all right, kid," announced Cairo. "Your Uncle Myron only left here a moment ago. He's walking, since he lost his wheels. Toward the ferryboat. I can still catch him for you, kid. Stay right here." The crow kicked the TV and it flickered on. "Don't move," he said. "Watch TV." He hopped off the lamp and headed for the open door of the motel room.

On screen a blond woman in a sweater set was being attacked by a swarm of birds. She screamed and held her hands in front of her face. Cairo T. paused in the doorway. "Hitchcock," he said to Billie, gesturing toward the television with his wing. *The Birds*. My ex-wife, Liz, is in this scene. She plays the seagull." With a flapping noise, he was gone.

The crow is being helpful after all, Billie thought. Maybe I misjudged him. As soon as he brings Uncle Myron back, everything will be okay. She looked at the screen. She'd seen this movie before in a hotel in

Pittsburgh. It was confusing. What was the problem with the birds supposed to be, anyway?

After a minute or so, a rumbling noise caught her attention. A car engine! Billie rushed to the doorway.

The Cadillac was rising into the air. Cairo T. Crow was behind the wheel. "Forgive me, kid!" he called down to Billie. The car swooped upward, sailing off into the night sky, tail fins silhouetted against the moon.

Wow! It can fly! Billie thought. That must be how Uncle Myron got us to this sleazy motel. Then another thought hit her. Bix was in there! Billie felt horribly afraid. This was the ultimate disaster. Bix had been kidnapped by a drunk driver while she'd been watching a Hitchcock movie.

She rushed back into Cairo's room and grabbed the telephone. Luckily, she had Mr. Eggwater's card in her pocket. The phone number of the Omaha Splendide Hotel was on the bottom. She dialed carefully, her hand shaking. It began to ring. What would she say to Mimi and Brian? "Listen, you're not gonna like this, but a crow stole Bix in a flying Cadillac. I was watching TV when it happened, but really—I'm a responsible kid. You can still trust me to baby-sit. By the way, do you think Uncle Myron has a gambling problem?"

A damp and burbly voice came on the line. "You have

reached the office of the Silver Moon Motel. Best in the Borderland. Switchboard is closed till pigs fly." A click, and the wet voice was gone.

Billie sat on the bed. The TV was still blaring, and the sound echoed into the dark night. Look at me, she thought. I wanted to get away from hotel rooms by running away, but even in a crazy country with flying cars and talking crows, I'm still stuck staring at floral bedspreads and white towels. I'm still watching TV and I'm still looking out the window at a landscape I don't recognize. Except this isn't the Princess Suite. And there's no Bix here to keep me company.

For the first time in her life, Billie felt so alone and confused she couldn't even cry.

4

Best Service Under the Moon

The sun was streaming through the Silver Moon Motel window. For a moment, when Billie awoke, she thought she was still on concert tour with her parents: another room in yet another city. Then the events of the day before came rushing back to her. It all seemed impossibly weird. Maybe I dreamed it, Billie thought. Then she saw the empty bottle of Strawberry Fizz on the floor alongside a black feather.

She walked outside onto the motel porch and sat down on the steps. The blue sky looked surprisingly ordinary, and so did the dusty desert landscape around the motel. I've got to find Bixie, she thought. For the first time it occurred to her that Mimi and Brian might be really worried. They had no way of finding out where she was. Uncle Myron didn't even know she and Bix had been in his car!

Glancing down, Billie noticed something bright orange at the bottom of the steps. A Cosmodemon figure lay there. It was bent and battered, covered with Bix's teeth marks. As she leaned down to pick it up, the ground moved under her hand! Billie grabbed the action figure by its orange horns before it could skitter away. The ground moved faster. Little tufts of grass zoomed past, along with bottle caps and old cigar wrappers. Then Billie realized it wasn't the ground moving at all—the whole motel was whizzing across the desert, floating about a foot off the ground.

Not only do I not know where I am, Billie thought, but now I don't know where I'm going. This place must have a concierge, or a clerk or something. She decided to head for the motel office and get some answers.

With the motel in violent zigzag motion, progress across the porch wasn't easy. It's a Tilt-A-Whirl, thought Billie, as she banged into the railing, grabbing a post to steady herself. It's a roller coaster! We must be going fifty miles an hour! A strong breeze whipped the sides of the building, and the wooden planks of the porch rumbled underneath her feet. Billie struggled to the office door and hung on to the knob for dear life, her hair flying in the wind. She knocked, banging away with her free hand.

"The office is closed till pigs fly," burbled a damp voice from behind the door. "Use the complaints box."

Billie looked everywhere. No box. She didn't know what good one would do if she found it. "There is no complaints box!" she shouted into the howling wind. "And you must be really nasty and horrible, whoever you are in that office, if you won't help a kid who's about to get blown off your crazy porch into the desert, where I'll get stuck on a cactus forever and die of thirst. LET ME IN!"

A fierce gust of wind suddenly blew the office door open and flung Billie inside. The door slammed shut behind her.

The Silver Moon office was entirely filled with sand. In the center of this sandpile, in a metal washtub by an old switchboard, was a very large clam. A high counter loomed behind it on which stood a bell and a chalkboard which read "Best Service Under the Moon."

"Rude little creature, aren't you?" asked the Clam in a deep, watery voice.

"Not at all," replied Billie angrily. "The wind blew me in here."

"That's what they all say."

The Clam was about three feet across and had a disgruntled look around the edges of its wavy mouth.

"Nearly crack myself open to provide fine service," it muttered, "and no one notices. No letter of thanks. No bubble bath." It let out a long sigh and then rose almost halfway up out of its washtub, as if staring at Billie, though where its eyes might be, she couldn't tell.

"I believe you're from the other side. Human," the Clam said in a far more genial tone. "Friend of the Kingfish?"

"Who's the Kingfish?" asked Billie.

"I love the Kingfish," continued the Clam. "He's a beautiful being."

"Who's the Kingfish?" asked Billie again.

"Did I hear you right, missie? You never heard of the Kingfish?"

"Never."

"The hell with the Kingfish," said the Clam with a burbly laugh. "Mommie Darling? You must be Mommie's little—"

"Mommie who?" interrupted Billie.

"Not Mommie, eh? Ah, Myron, then!" the Clam said with conviction.

"He's my uncle."

"What's your name, missie?" demanded the Clam.

"Billie. Like the singer Billie Holiday."

"Well, Missie Holiday, your Uncle Myron is a regular customer. What say you and me go out on the porch for a little air and cream soda, now that the old Silver Moon has slowed down. If you'll just grab this handle here . . ."

Billie took the metal handle and pulled the washtub out onto the porch. The motel was still moving, but at a calm and steady pace. The wind had become a gentle breeze. The Clam splashed and gurgled contentedly as two bottles of cream soda bobbed to the surface from the icy bottom of his bath.

"Help yourself, missie," said the Clam, "and help me, too. I can't handle those twist-offs." Billie opened both bottles and poked the end of one down into the Clam's mouth.

"Ah, cream soda! Every clam's favorite. Just relax, Missie Holiday, and watch those cacti whiz by!"

"Uh, just where is this motel going?"

The Clam snorted, and the curves of its mouth wiggled slightly in amusement. "You don't know much about traveling, do you, Missie Holiday?"

"That's one thing I do know about," Billie protested. "I know all the room service waiters in the fanciest hotels. I know all my state capitals. I've even been to Europe five times."

"Hah!" barked the Clam. "Traveling between places that stand still is child's play. In the Borderland, things are changing too fast for that kind of slowpoke-a-motion. All wiggling and ziggling. The Silver Moon serves the Borderland. Right now we're traveling along the edge of the Endless Desert, missie, the great sandy space that's in between the Borderland and everyplace else. Ziggle-zaggle!"

Here the Clam paused till it had sucked the cream soda dry. Billie politely removed the bottle. "We stop in a new and restful location every sunset," the Clam continued. "Don't want to travel at night. Dangerous darkness in the Borderland, missie. Wild nightlife."

"I'm not scared of nightlife," said Billie. "I go to rock shows all the time. I even went to a Grammy Awards party. I drank a virgin piña colada and stayed up past midnight."

"Nevertheless," said the Clam, with a particular burbliness in its voice, "you'll need insurance."

"Uh, you wouldn't know where my Uncle Myron is right now, would you?" asked Billie, trying to change the subject.

"No idea," rumbled the Clam. "But if you want to find someone in the Borderland, you'll *certainly* need insurance."

"Insurance for what?"

"INSURANCE," roared the Clam, banging against the metal edges of the tub in its excitement, "against the unforeseeable. INSURANCE against the unexpected.

INSURANCE against the unexplainable." The Clam spun about in its tub. "I'm a salesclam, young lady, and what I'm selling, a traveler like you should not be without. I can give you the deal of a lifetime!"

"I don't think I can buy anything," said Billie. She looked down into her plastic purse. "All I have is a tangerine lip gloss and a peanut butter and Marshmallow Fluff sandwich."

"Peanut butter and Fluff? My favorite! Marshmallows are impossible to find in the Borderland. The Kingfish keeps them all in his palace."

"Who's this Kingfish you keep talking about?"

"He puts them on top of his"—the Clam's voice sank to a bubbly whisper—"pudding. I'll take it!"

"You want my sandwich? But it's all I've got left to eat. I don't want to starve out here in the desert."

"Missie, this is a deal for you at any price. Come on. Let me have that Marshmallow Fluff! Let me have it, and insure yourself, young lady!"

Reluctantly, Billie unwrapped her sandwich and slipped it gently between the Clam's wavy lips. The peanut butter and Fluff on whole wheat disappeared with a gentle sucking sound. The Clam gurgled with delight.

A round plastic medallion floated to the surface of the water. It was on a chain, like a necklace, and had the word INSURANCE printed on it in large purple letters. "It's all yours, missie," said the Clam. "Put it on."

Billie slipped the wet necklace over her head. As she did so, the motel jerked to a halt near a large pond, surrounded by marshy grass. "Why are we stopping?" asked Billie.

"Repairs," the Clam told her. "It's an old motel. It breaks down occasionally. Must be a spark plug. C'mon, missie, you don't think I can do it myself, do you? Tip it over!"

"Tip what over?" asked Billie, a little annoyed. The Clam was bossy in the extreme.

"My washtub, missie!" Billie grabbed the iron handles and tilted the tub forward. With a great gush of water, the Clam slid out, down the steps, and onto the ground in front of the motel. Now that she could see it better, Billie was less impressed. The Clam seemed smaller, and evidently it was its own billboard. Lettering covered the entire top of its shell. "Accident Insurance. Loneliness Insurance. French Test Insurance. Claims settled promptly. Open 24 hours . . ." There was more to read, but before Billie could finish, the Clam began to wriggle underneath the porch with a slurpy rolling motion.

"I'll be just a minute," it called from underneath the

motel. Billie could hear the sound of metal tools clanking together. Where had the clam been keeping them? Inside its shell? A few minutes later, a slightly greasy Clam wriggled back into the sunshine. It held a wrench in one corner of its mouth.

"Can't afford a breakdown, missie," it remarked. "Got an insurance convention checking in this evening. Shellfish Mutual. Now I gotta get myself cleaned up. Help me back in there, missie, and add water. Moisture's a necessity, you know, at my age."

Following instructions, Billie lifted the Clam gently back into the tub and dragged it inside the office. On the counter was a large jug of water. She poured it with a splash onto the Clam's painted shell, rinsing the motor oil off the advertisement.

"You're a helpful young thing," the Clam remarked when it was well settled. "Ever been a maid? We've got a job open here at the Silver Moon, you know. Room service, moisture maintenance, that sort of thing."

"No way," snapped Billie. "I'm not a maid."

"What's wrong with being a maid?" grumbled the Clam. "It's no disgrace. Think you're too good for it, do you, missie? Think you can run about the world playing and partying and never clean up after yourself?" Billie didn't know what to say, and after a moment, the Clam continued. "If you don't want the job, this is your stop. Business is business. I got that convention."

"What should I do?" asked Billie, not wanting to be left alone.

"Take the Showboat. Fast and cheap. Off you go."

"The Showboat?" She wasn't sure what the Clam meant, but the creature was starting to get impatient. "Thank you," she said politely. "Good-bye."

Billie stepped out onto the porch and down to the edge of the pond. The motel, with a clatter of room keys and squeals from the remaining tenants, began to move again. Billie watched it pick up speed. A spray of sand and water erupted out of the office window. "So long, young missie," the Clam's voice burbled. "Remember! Best Service Under the Moon."

The waters of the pond rippled and sparkled in the sun. She was really all alone now.

Where was Bix? She reached into her purse and held the chewed-up orange action figure tight in her hand. This was all her fault. He was only two years old. Did he have any pudding? Was he lonely, too?

5

The Great Nostromo

"Step aside!" piped a high voice from right behind Billie. She turned around and nearly stepped on a large family of field mice. A fat father mouse was shaking his paw at her. The children were wearing sun hats and carrying lunch boxes. Billie made way and the whole group pushed anxiously into a line that was rapidly forming at the edge of the shore.

Chugging across the pond was a huge white Mississippi steamboat, belching bright pink smoke from its twin funnels. Billie could hear the merry sound of ragtime piano music. The great paddle spun into reverse, and the boat glided smoothly to a stop a little way out from shore. A boarding ramp extended from its side. The field mice rushed up the plank and on deck, followed by a stream of creatures, with more pouring down from nearby trees and crawling from small holes in the ground. They were mainly woodland animals: badgers, beavers, porcupines, and otters. Some were carrying gaily decorated picnic hampers.

This is like the small mammal house at the zoo and a huge community picnic combined, thought Billie. She'd never actually been to a community picnic. She'd only read about them in books. There are no community picnics when you live in a different hotel every week.

"Well," she said to herself, "I don't want to be left here on the edge of the Endless Desert. Maybe one of the creatures on the Showboat can help me find Bixie."

She boarded and found a good spot along one rail. A great horn sounded and the Showboat pulled away from shore, billowing pink smoke. It headed for the far end of the pond. Next to her was a fat white duck in a chaise longue.

Why would a duck need to ride a steamboat? Can't he swim? wondered Billie. She tapped the duck on one wing. "Excuse me," she said, "I'm looking for my little brother. Have you noticed a sticky-faced two-year-old human anywhere?"

"*Mademoiselle, je ne parle jamais avec les étrangers humains*," replied the Duck, smoothing his shiny white feathers.

What was he saying? Great, Billie thought. Even in this crazy Borderland I can't escape French.

"Je déteste les enfants," quacked the Duck. Billie understood enough to know that *enfants* meant children and she figured *déteste* meant detest. How rude. She couldn't remember enough French to talk back.

"Feather duster," she said, sneering at the Duck, remembering the effect of this phrase on Cairo T. Crow.

"Pardon?"

She tried it in her best French accent: "Featherrr dustehhrrr."

The Duck did not respond.

"Duck à l'orange!" Billie shouted the first French words that came into her head. She had eaten it once for dinner in a restaurant in Paris. Abruptly, the nasty duck heaved himself out of the chaise longue and waddled off to the other side of the boat, ruffling his feathers and quacking under his breath.

The sound of the piano grew louder. Looking around, Billie noticed she was now the only passenger on deck. Where had everyone gone? The music was coming from behind a pair of double doors. On them was painted in large gold letters:

THE GREAT NOSTROMO,

PRESTIDIGITATOR EXTRAORDINAIRE!

EXTREMELY WONDROUS! SUPERBLY CHARMING!

HOTTER THAN TABASCO SAUCE!

Billie pushed through the doors and found herself at the back of a crowded theater, the stage masked by a red velvet curtain. She was also face-to-face with a warty frog and a wrinkly elephant, sitting alongside a table with an open cigar box on it. The elephant, wearing thick spectacles and a pink tutu, smiled at Billie pleasantly and returned to her work. She was carefully darning the tutu she wore, holding a needle adeptly in her trunk. The frog was sitting on the elephant's knee wearing a coat made of a plastic bag on which were stuck a lot of paper stars. Its head was covered with a golden paper crown, on which the words BEST IN SHOW were clearly visible.

"Pay up, my dear," said the Frog. "We don't make fools of ourselves for free."

"I don't have any money," Billie said nervously.

"Money?" laughed the Frog. "Nobody's got any money."

"Nobody but the Kingfish," muttered the elephant under her breath.

"Look at the price of a ticket these days!" cried the Frog. Billie looked in the cigar box: half a frankfurter, a spool of thread, an old copy of *TV Guide*, a screwdriver, some wildflowers, and various other odd or useless items. She got her tangerine lip gloss out of her purse and dropped it in. With a hungry glint in his eye, the

Frog leaped in after it, popped the cap, and took a neat little bite off the end. He smacked his lips.

"Not bad, sweetheart. I'm King Buster, the emcee. King of the Ukulele." The Frog puffed himself up with pride. "This is my wife, the Great Madame Zanoni!" The elephant lumbered to her feet and delicately offered her trunk for Billie to shake. Billie shook it, and was surprised at how soft it felt.

"I'm Billie."

"Glad to make your acquaintance," croaked King Buster. "And who's the orange monster peeking out of your purse?"

"It's a Cosmodemon," Billie said, holding up the tooth-marked figure. "It belongs to my little brother Bix."

"How old is he?" asked Madame Zanoni kindly.

"Two."

"I'll let him in free!" cried King Buster, hopping up and down with joy at his own generosity.

"He isn't here," said Billie sadly. "He's lost."

"That's too bad," said King Buster.

"So am I," Billie continued. "I'm lost, too."

"That's even worse," sighed the Frog, looking at Madame Zanoni for confirmation. "An entire lost family."

"Not quite," said Billie. "My uncle—" She was interrupted by a loud drumroll from onstage.

"Uh-oh," the Frog croaked. "That's my cue."

Madame Zanoni, looking a little frazzled, was already lumbering through a side door. "Catch you after the show, Billie!" called King Buster, hopping after his wife. "Maybe we can help you out!"

"Wait!" she cried, but they were gone.

Billie found her way down the aisle and sat down. The lights dimmed, and the red velvet curtain opened. King Buster was perched on a stool, holding a ukulele. He played a wild sequence of riffs, hopping madly up and down and grinning. He closed with a flourish, stretching his warty body up to its full height.

"Ladies and gentlemen!" King Buster shouted. "Our featured attraction, the favorite of creatures large and small, a hit in swamp, town, and woodland—the GREAT NOSTROMO!" He whacked his ukulele a good one.

There was a wonderful puff of smoke, and out of it stepped a man in a flame-red cape, a top hat, and a huge mustache. The audience applauded, and a baby woodchuck seated near Billie, overcome by the special effects, hid his furry face in his mother's apron. Billie almost fell out of her chair. The man in the cape was her Uncle Myron!

She was totally relieved. Her troubles were over. She knew they were. She'd wait until the show was finished, and then she'd make her way backstage. No problem.

Ever since she was five years old, she'd been pushing past screaming fans to get to Mimi's dressing room. That was probably the stage door, there to the left of the curtain. Finding Myron would be easy.

Billie sat back to enjoy the show. Uncle Myron, alias the Great Nostromo, was fantastic. Flowers came out of his sleeves. A kangaroo came out of his silk top hat. Monkeys emerged magically from his pockets and crawled over his broad shoulders. As a finale, he levitated, floating three feet off the ground. Then, with a flourish of his red silk cape, Uncle Myron disappeared in a puff of smoke. The audience applauded wildly, squawking and chattering with enthusiasm. The baby woodchuck nearly passed out from excitement.

King Buster returned to the stage, strummed his ukulele, and shouted, "Let's welcome, in her *Dance to Springtime*, the ever-elegant Madame Zanoni!"

Madame Zanoni, her gray skin hanging in huge wrinkly folds all over her body, glided to the center of the stage. She still wore her eyeglasses, and her ratty pink tutu was covered with patches. On her feet were enormous pink ballet shoes. She curtsied, and when the sprightly music started up, she began to dance in little hopping steps. *Thump! Ka-thump!* She was so heavy she shook the stage. The floorboards bent and creaked under her weight. The audience booed and hooted.

The young woodchuck poked his mother in the side. "Ma," he asked, "that ballerina's really old, isn't she?"

"Hush!" his mother said. "Madame Zanoni is still queen of them all. Her dying swan has never been matched."

A tall stork behind Billie whispered audibly to her companion, "That elephant shouldn't be performing. She's long past her prime. A travesty."

One rowdy group of young porcupines heaved some overripe tomatoes at the stage. King Buster hopped forward, shouting, "Cut that out, you spiny little brats!"

The porcupines let a few more fly. An especially rotten one squished on Madame Zanoni's tutu, leaving a red stain. The dignified performer didn't even blink. She danced on. Billie thought it was awfully rude to throw the tomatoes, but she could see why they were flying. It was the most terrible dancing she'd ever seen, though she could tell that once, maybe long ago, these same steps were light and graceful. As the music surged, Madame Zanoni took an especially daring leap upward and landed with an enormous *thunk*. Her forelegs crashed through the floor, splinters and wood flying. The poor thing struggled, but the hole only grew bigger, and then, to everyone's complete amazement,

Madame Zanoni disappeared through the broken floor of the stage!

A huge fountain of water flooded up through the hole. She'd not only broken through the stage, but through the bottom of the boat. They were sinking!

Bells began to clang, and all the creatures rushed for the exits. Billie was knocked over by the mother woodchuck, pushing up the aisle with her child under her arm. She scrambled to her feet and shouted, "Uncle Myron! Uncle Myron!"

The room was a chaotic mass of squealing creatures, and the air was filled with the flapping of wings. An anxious Great Dane shoved Billie in the shoulder as it bounded over the seats toward the main doors. She looked at the stage. Myron's crimson cape lay on the floorboards next to the enormous hole made by Madame Zanoni. Had he fallen in? She couldn't see him anywhere. The water in the theater was up to Billie's knees, and the animals were panicking. She had to get out on deck.

"Uncle Myron!" she called again as she waded up the aisle, grabbing on to the backs of the velvet seats to pull herself forward. No answer. Finally she reached the deck and staggered to the rail of the sinking Showboat. All around her the passengers were diving over the side and swimming for shore. The field mice were clinging nervously to the back of the fat French duck as it balanced on the railing, ready to plunge into the waves. The Great Dane was dog-paddling in the water with two meowing kittens perched on its head. She looked frantically for Uncle Myron, but he was nowhere to be found.

I'm gonna drown! she thought. We're going down like the *Titanic*. We'll be written up in the history books: *Sunk by a fat elephant, the wreckage of the Showboat counted no survivors.* Years from now, divers will look for treasure in the remains of the ship! I'll be down at the bottom of the pond like Davy Jones and his locker, whatever that is. My eyes will turn into pearls and I'll puff up and turn blue and someone will find me and look through my pockets. What a horrible end! "Uncle MYRON!" she cried desperately.

By this time, most of the animals had jumped over the side of the boat. It was quiet on deck. A few dogs and other animals who swam well were collecting the last few tiny creatures in baskets and preparing to carry them to safety. Now that the panic was over, Billie realized she could see the shoreline not far away. She calmed down a bit. She wasn't going to drown at all, just get wet. It was an easy distance.

Making sure her purse was tied to her belt with a piece of string, Billie dove over the side and hit the water with a splash. Coming to the surface, she spotted one of the double doors from the theater entrance bobbing nearby, its gold paint glinting in the sun. She grabbed on to it with both hands and pulled herself aboard. She could use it as a raft and paddle to the beach.

The abandoned Showboat sank into the depths. Billie had been the last to leave the wreck, and as she floated away from it, she could see some animals emerge on shore, shake themselves dry, and disappear into the forest. Was that Myron's top hat heading into the woods? She couldn't be sure.

"MYRON!" she yelled as loud as she could. "Uncle Myron! Nostromo! I'm over here!" But Uncle Myron, if that's who it was, couldn't hear her. In a moment the figure on the shore was out of sight.

"Did you say the Great Nostromo is your uncle?" The question came from a wet rabbit with an earring in one ear who floated on a nearby chunk of stage floor. "Nostromo is entirely cool," said the rabbit. "He'd never be allowed to perform in the city these days. His mind, you know, it's totally open. Freedom! Love! Nature! He's the real thing."

"Real what?" asked Billie.

"Freedom! Love! Nature!" The rabbit paused. "He's your uncle, you say?"

"Of course not," snapped an authoritative voice. Billie turned. Floating in the pond was a watermelon, carved like a jack-o'-lantern with a wide, toothy smile. "This innocent kid is completely unrelated to Nostromo," cried the watermelon. "She's my secretary, Penelope Prunebottom. We're taking notes for a hot story on the Showboat disaster: 'Terror on the Pond.'" The rabbit looked disappointed and floated swiftly off in the opposite direction. The watermelon continued to shout—"Come on, Penelope! Paddle, paddle!"—until the rabbit was out of sight.

The melon sunk underwater for a moment, and then, with a great splash, the oddest contraption Billie had ever seen heaved itself up and landed dripping on the floating door. Someone had attached a TV camera to the top of an electric wheelchair. Mechanical gizmos and computer circuit boards were wired in all over it. On top of the camera was the carved watermelon, mounted horizontally. That same someone had taken a great deal of care with the face. It had a jovial, dimpled look, set off by fierce, determined eyebrows. A homemade robot.

Billie paddled the last few feet to the beach.

"Kent here. Live from the shore," announced the robot as it rolled off the wet door onto solid ground. "Don't worry about me. I'm equipped for disasters of all sorts. Totally waterproof! Dry yourself off. There's a towel under my seat." And so there was, in a little plastic pouch that also contained some lubricating oil and a few tiny tools.

"Thank you." Billie began to dry her hair.

"You're welcome. Are you really related to Nostromo?" the robot asked, his zoom lens zeroing in on her face.

"He's my Uncle Myron."

"Keep it under wraps. Nostromo is *not* in favor with the Kingfish. Not in favor at all." He leaned precariously toward Billie and whispered in her ear. He smelled like a mixture of watermelon and gasoline. "The Kingfish tried to have him arrested on charges of Public Entertainment and Unlawful Possession of Marshmallows, but he escaped in that fishtail Cadillac convertible. He hasn't set foot in Donuthole since then, and that was almost a year ago. Any relation of his better be careful."

"What's Donuthole?"

"It's the big city in the middle of the Borderland, like the hole in the middle of a donut."

"And who's the Kingfish?" asked Billie.

"Shhhhh! Someone might hear us."

"Well, then, who are you?"

"I'm Clark Kent, roving reporter. Call me Clark. I serve Mommie Darling, mechanical genius and inventor. She got into bed ten years ago and never got out. She's comfortable in there, but she misses knowing the latest scoop. Likes to be up on things. So she made me. I'm half TV studio and half electric rolling chair. I broadcast back to Mommie. Whatever I see, she sees back home on her TV. She's looking at you right now."

"Hi!" Billie waved at the camera.

"No use waiting for an answer," said Clark. "Mommie Darling can't reply. No feedback. I am on a programmed mission. If I don't give her what she wants, she calls me in for repairs and fiddles with my circuitry. She likes junk food and junk TV. Today I almost drowned, but I got fabulous coverage of the Showboat disaster. A sensation! That's all Mommie likes. Action. Violence. And a little kissing."

"Ugh," groaned Billie.

"That's what I think, too," agreed Clark, "but a job's a job."

They were at the foot of some low gray hills covered with plum-colored trees. It was beautiful, but quiet and a little spooky. A wide dirt path stretched off into the distance.

"I've got to get moving," continued the reporter. "Mommie hates scenery, and that's all this place has got. If I stay too long gazing at the beauties of the landscape, trying to convey the indescribable poignancy of the natural world through the highly artificial medium of videography, she calls me into her workshop for repairs. Good-bye, Billie. Nice to know you."

"Don't leave me here!" Billie cried. "I'm in trouble! How will I get home?" Clark Kent kept rolling away from her. "Wait! If you give me a ride, you're sure to find some action."

"What kind?" asked Clark, stopping suddenly and turning his watermelon head. "Mommie's particular."

"How's cheating at Old Maid?"

"Nothing special."

"Auto theft?"

"Better."

"Kidnapping of defenseless human babies?"

"Now you're talking!" cried Clark. "Let's hit the road."

6

Spawned to Be Wild

Billie never knew wheelchairs could go so fast. Riding on Clark Kent was like driving with Brian, who loved to get behind the wheel. He and Billie had rented a dune buggy last summer on the beach. The sun was shining, and Bix and Mimi had lounged in a rubber boat pulled up on the sand. Brian had driven the buggy much too fast. He'd waved his hat in the air and hollered like a cowboy, and the wind had whizzed through Billie's hair. She closed her eyes and felt the wind in her hair again as Clark Kent sped through the boring scenery toward something Mommie Darling would find more stimulating.

Suddenly the robot stopped short, flinging Billie out of his wheelchair seat onto the hard ground.

"Watch it, melonhead!" she yelled, standing up and

brushing dirt off her jeans. Then she realized that Clark Kent was quivering all over, the way Bixie did when he met a dog larger than he was. Large poodles with fancy hairdos scared him the most. Once Billie had carried him around for a whole afternoon after a particularly close encounter with Roberta's dog, Fang.

"Shhh!" hissed Clark. "Listen!" He shook so hard that his loose metal parts clanked together.

"What's wrong?" Billie asked.

"Shhhh!" Clark Kent whispered again. "Groupers!"

Billie listened. In the distance she heard the roar of engines, coming closer.

"What are Groupers?" she asked.

"Take cover!" Clark whispered. "Quickly!" He drove himself into some bushes, rustling the leaves around him until he was completely hidden.

Billie scrambled into the bushes as the roar got louder. She crouched by the reporter's right wheel and peeked out through the leaves. "Kent here. Live from a bush," he whispered. "Action potential, high. Possible violent crimes."

Six shiny chrome motorcycles, choppers, zoomed into view and Billie gasped with surprise. Perched on each seat was a huge, silver-scaled fish. They were enormous, each about three hundred pounds of solid muscle. Their tail fins did not quite reach the kick-starter, and they seemed to operate the cycles with their front flippers wrapped tightly around the handlebars.

Each Grouper had a large scuba tank strapped to its back, painted with a skull and crossbones. They wore huge diving helmets, which fitted tightly over their heads and gills, and were connected to the tanks with thick black tubes. Inside the helmets their fishy faces swam in a sea of bubbling water.

The lead motorcycle spun in a circle and screeched to a stop. The fish driving it leaned back in his seat and polished his handlebars with an oily fin as the five other cycles drove up and cut their engines.

"Hatched to Ride!" cried the leader, punching his fin into the air.

"Hatched to Ride!" cried the others, doing likewise.

"Spawned to Be Wild!" yelled the smallest Grouper, who was riding last in the pack. He punched both fins high in gleeful villainy.

"Shut your gills, Luther," growled the leader. "Now listen up. We're looking for a girl. A human girl. No scales, no fur, no fins. Ugly, puny, and spoiled rotten. Last spotted on the Showboat. Possibly drowned, but more likely out making trouble."

"Hey, Archibald," Luther piped up, "I got a question."

Archibald grunted with exasperation. "You're thinking again, Luther. Thinking's not your job."

"What does the Kingfish want with her, Archibald?"

"Be careful, Luther, or your water-breather will be
on the scrap heap and you'll be back in the pond.
Search the area!" he ordered the gang. "If you find her,
squish her pronto! Bonus from the Kingfish to the one
who brings her in, flat as a pancake!"

With a roar of engines, the cycles zoomed off,
Luther tagging along in the rear, a little unsteady on his
two wheels.

A hush descended on the uninteresting scenery. Billie crawled out of the bush. Clark Kent, trailing a few
leaves, drove nervously into the clearing. He still
looked so shaky that Billie felt sorry for him, even
though he was just a machine.

"They're a gang, right?" asked Billie. "Or are they
the police?"

"They're both," answered Clark. "Rumor has it that
the Groupers hail from the long-lost city of Atlantis
Others say they grew huge because of the toxic wast
dumped into the big pond a few years back. Aquam
rine assassins. Would-be amphibians. They work {
the Kingfish. He invented their water-breathers. Th
scuba tanks are filled with water, not air. That's }
they breathe on land."

"Why are they looking for me?"

"I don't know. I don't want to know," replied Clark nervously. "Even Mommie Darling doesn't want to know."

"Why are you so afraid of them?"

"Me? Afraid?" snapped Clark. "I am a busy and high-tech piece of journalistic equipment. No time for emotions. I was *not* afraid. Totally impossible. It's not in my programming."

"Okay, okay," answered Billie, seeing she'd hit a sensitive circuit. "But what do they do that...uh... might frighten someone else?"

"They'll squish you. Lie on top of you. Three hundred pounds of smelly, oily fish, overpowering you with odor and slowly, agonizingly squishing the life from your frail mammal body." The reporter paused for dramatic effect. "They have another terrible talent: The Groupers wield insults like butcher knives. Name-calling, beyond the feeble nastiness you hear on the playground, Billie. The Groupers can bad-mouth a person practically out of existence. The heat of their scorn would make even Elvis feel unloved. As a matter of fact, King Buster the emcee was the victim of one of the most notorious Grouper attacks ever."

"King Buster, really?" cried Billie, remembering the talkative frog playing ukulele in the magic show.

"Yes, King Buster. The Groupers hate real amphibians. They're jealous of any animal who can live naturally both on land and in the water. They circled around him, slowly. 'Wartface!' they yelled. 'Bug-eater! Your ukulele playing sounds like the lonely snorts of love-starved rhinoceri in Bogbottom Swamp. Your wife is a wrinkly bag of elephant blubber! Back to the pond! BACK TO THE POND!' Then they—ahh, but the rest is not for children to hear. King Buster turned purple with frustration and then white with shame. It took him months in a clinic to regain his normal green color, and his sense of dignity never did quite come back."

Thinking of King Buster and his nearsighted wife, Billie became angry. "Those bullies!" she cried. "Next time I see them, I'll eat them for dinner. I'll grill them all on the barbecue, marinated in teriyaki. No, no, I'll squeeze lemon juice on them and make a little tartar sauce to go on the side. No! Even better! I'll feed the poor with them, and give the bones to starving alley cats."

She was about to continue, and in fact was only beginning to work herself up, when she was interrupted by a rustling in the tree above her head.

Somewhere in the universe, a strange woman was in bed watching TV. It was Mommie Darling, and she had just tuned in. "A human child," she commented aloud to Fixit, her electronic handyman and chef. "At last that reporter is doing his job. Remember three days ago when he spent hours in that field of marigolds? Clark's artistic inclinations had gone totally out of control. I was sure there was something wrong with him. I was so disgusted with his pretentious nature documentaries that I haven't watched since. But now he's delivering according to program. A sweet little girl, lost in the woods. What kind of action can we get here? Maybe she'll get eaten by a wolf. Or run over by a bus!"

"Mommie," admonished Fixit, "you don't really want that to happen."

"True enough." Mommie sighed, biting into a slice of chocolate cake. "Maybe she'll kiss a frog and miracles will occur."

"That'd be nice," Fixit said.

"No, it wouldn't," decided Mommie fretfully. "Kissing always reminds me of Herman Mudhen, my ex-husband. Did I ever tell you about him, Fixit?" But Fixit, who hung from the ceiling like a chandelier, quickly pulled himself up into the attic space where his kitchen equipment was. He was not a machine designed for sympathy. He rattled the pans around loudly, indicating that he was not available to hear the sad story of Mr. Mudhen.

Mommie searched for a napkin in the pile of magazines, dirty dishes, and electronic equipment that filled her giant bed. "I'll have to reprogram Fixit someday," she muttered to herself. "I never should have made him such a practical gadget. I could make a great companion out of him with just a few new chips, but he always pulls up out of reach when I get the welder out." She turned her attention back to the television. The image on the giant screen had changed. Instead of the interesting human child, a mass of foliage was rustling violently. What was Clark Kent looking at now?

7

Bird Bar

"'Snot-for-brains! Droolie-schoolie! Nerd-nose!'" The voice sobbing these strange phrases came from a mass of foliage overhead. Billie looked up as Clark's camera zoomed in. Hanging from a tree limb was a bony goat wearing a polka-dot housedress and a moth-eaten beaded sweater. She was crying. One of her tears dripped onto Billie's shoe.

"'Irrelevant and shallow,' they called me. 'Four eyes! Old Maid!'" The goat paused in her weepy catalog of insults. "Are those sea-scum gone?"

"The Groupers?" said Billie. "I think so."

The goat sighed with relief. She slid down the trunk of the tree and stood before them. Her eyes were red behind thick glasses. "I told them," she babbled. "I shouted! NO TALKING NEAR THE LIBRARY!"

"We're in the middle of a forest," said Billie. "What library?"

"Me. Your Library Goat, at your service. I recited something I thought they'd like: *The History of Finland.* They revved their monstrous motorcycles and laughed. A horrible burbly-wurbly laugh. My literacy was a joke to them." Your Library Goat broke into tears again, her whole body shaking. After a moment, she pulled a huge red handkerchief from her pocket and noisily blew her nose.

"Kent here. Live from the forest depths." Clark's camera followed the goat's every move. "Ace reporter discovers Goat Library!"

"Some sort of electromechanical contrivance, aren't you?" asked Your Library Goat.

"What of it?" Clark replied, zooming the goat into close-up. "Do you have a problem with that?"

"Contrivances can be as ignorant as creatures." She waggled one hoof vigorously at the rambling reporter. "Don't neglect your child's education, mister. I myself was a kindergarten dropout. I watched cartoons and ate dandelions. My brain had turned completely into green Jell-O when I saw the error of my ways. I began to exert myself. Starting with Book A of the encyclopedia, 'Aardvark to Aztec,' I spent every moment in pursuit of knowledge." The goat paused to look hard at Billie. "Why aren't *you* in school, dear?"

"I don't go to school. I have a tutor."

"Then you'll need to use the library. It's in my head. I have committed ten thousand volumes to memory. Recitation on request. No need for a rubber stamp saying 'Property of Donuthole Public Library.' I'm convenient and I'm portable. What's your reading level?"

"I don't have a reading level," said Billie. "I can read anything—almost."

"Head of the class! How about *The Phenomenology of Grammatology*? It's my longest, and it's partly in Latin. It'll take only a few weeks."

Billie didn't have a few weeks, or even a few days. For all she knew, she didn't even have a few hours. "Have you seen a dirty-faced two-year-old kid?" she asked. "Answers to Bix? Bixie? He's my little brother, and I've got to find him or my parents will kill me. If I ever get back to them. Besides, he might be scared. Or hungry. Or worse."

"Sorry, my dear."

"Do you know my Uncle Myron?"

"The Great Nostromo?" interrupted Clark Kent. The goat just shook her head.

"Do you know a Cairo T. Crow?" pleaded Billie.

"Red eyes? Leather cap? Greasy feathers?" This time Your Library Goat looked thoughtful. Then her eyes brightened.

"I need some refreshment," she said. "Join me, my loyal readership. As we go, I will begin *The Phenomenology of Grammatology*, a work of undeniable virtue." She turned suddenly and headed rapidly down the path, trotting and reciting at once. "The theoretical examination of the function of reflexive signifiers exemplifies in itself the impossibility of actual communication. However, this need not stop us. Deconstructing the . . ." In a moment she was out of earshot. Billie leaped into Clark Kent's lap, and they followed her. Your Library Goat might be boring, but at least she wasn't lost.

Sooner than Billie expected, the trio came out of the forest and into a wide meadow. In it stood a building that looked exactly like a huge upside-down bird's nest. Your Library Goat headed right for the door, made of mud and straw, on which was hung a sign: BIRD BAR.

They went in. Billie had been in bars with her parents, but this one was bright pink inside, and decorated entirely with large photographs of eggs. All the customers were birds of various kinds, including a crowd of very noisy pigeons. The whole place resounded with squawking and chirping. Your Library Goat led them to a table at the rear. Clark Kent was delighted, his camera wheeling and swiveling.

"Kent here. Live from the Bird Bar," he announced, focusing on a lean vulture and a blue peacock dancing beak to beak on a tabletop. "Mommie'll love this place."

A large white bird of a kind Billie had never seen before came toward them. She was wearing an apron. "Albatross," said Your Library Goat, before Billie could ask.

"What'll it be?" said the albatross. Clark Kent pointed his camera at her. He reminded Billie of one of those paparazzi who followed Mimi and Brian everywhere.

"A large Strawberry Fizz, my dear," said Your Library Goat.

"Do you have any pudding?" Billie asked, thinking of Bix. Suddenly, all the squawking and chirping stopped. You could hear a feather drop. The albatross leaned over the table, her huge yellow beak almost in Billie's face.

"Never say 'pudding' in my place again, young lady. It reminds everyone of things they'd rather forget. I'll bring you a nice dish of worms."

The albatross wheeled off toward the kitchen before Billie could stop her. As the Bird Bar returned to its normal level of chatter, a particularly large buzzard appeared in the doorway. He was a balding bird with a paunchy, molting stomach, smoking a large cigar. Billie watched as he glided over to the albatross, pinching her tail feathers.

"Dolores," he said. "*Enchanté*, my downy duckling." He threw his cashmere coat over Dolores's arm and headed for a corner table. This table was covered with empty bottles of Strawberry Fizz. Underneath it lay a bird, sleeping it off. He wore a leather cap.

The buzzard gave the slumped figure a sharp kick in the claw. "Rise and shine, my little companion of the night. We have an appointment with destiny."

The bird awoke with a squawk, and stared up at the buzzard with red-rimmed eyes. He struggled to his feet and waved one greasy black wing.

"Oh my gosh!" said Billie, nudging Clark. "It's that crow! Cairo T.! He drove into the sky with Bix!" She marched right over to the crow and the buzzard, with Clark Kent close behind her. "Where's my little brother?" she asked the crow in what she hoped was a very stern voice. The buzzard removed the cigar from his beak, blew a perfect smoke ring toward the ceiling, and grabbed Billie's hand with one wing. He gave her a delicate peck on the knuckle.

"Miss Billie? *Enchanté!*" said the bird. Its voice was

throaty and cultivated. "I'm Bernard Buzzard. My companion and I have been hoping to meet you. Haven't we, Crow?" The crow looked at Billie, sucked the last drop out of a bottle of Strawberry Fizz, and leapt up onto the table. He began to sing while dancing a little two-step.

> *There once was a seagull named Liz,*
> *Who had glamorous dreams of show biz.*
> *I worshipped that gull,*
> *But she thought I was dull.*
> *Now I swim in a river of Fizz.*

He stopped singing and looked at Billie sadly. A huge tear rolled down his cheek.

"You're crying," said Billie, "and you've had too much of that pink stuff."

"Drowning my sorrows," said the crow. "I lost your brother, kid! Bixie, what a lad! That Cadillac didn't like me, you know. Myron warned me. It kept doing three-sixtys, flipping me out of the driver's seat. Won it fair and square, but it was so much trouble I had to dump it in the middle of Bogbottom Swamp. I was walking away when I heard a little cry from the backseat. I looked, and there he was. BIX! A boy among boys. I gave him a lollipop."

"He gave him a *huge* lollipop," said Bernard Buzzard, blowing another smoke ring. "Enormous."

"I left him on a bench near a phone booth," said the crow in a weepy voice. "I told him to sit tight while I made a few calls. I was trying to find out where the young cutie belonged. When I got back to the bench, little Bix was gone."

"Gone, but not forgotten," said the buzzard, with a throb in his voice. He blew a double smoke ring, a perfect figure eight.

"I've got to find him. He can't survive on his own. He's only two! He can't even speak English, and he *must* be starving." Billie whispered the rest in the buzzard's ear. "All he'll eat is pudding."

Bernard whispered back, "Pudding, eh? Far be it from me, of course, to say where your brother might be. However, I've heard a rumor that the Kingfish has access to a certain amount of pudding. A *certain* amount, my dear. I've even heard that when the Kingfish likes someone, he lets them stay in the palace. They can stay forever and ever. Even if they want to go home."

"How do I get to see this Kingfish?" asked Billie.

"I'll take you," offered the crow. "It'll make up for my losing Bix. What a lad!"

"No thanks. You can just give us directions." Clark

Kent, who had overheard everything, interrupted the crow. "I'll get us to this Kingfish without your help. I'm a highly sophisticated piece of journalistic equipment."

"You can't walk into the palace just like that, Vid-head," snapped Cairo. "It's right in the middle of Donuthole. There are Groupers everywhere. You need to find the secret entrance. You need to know the password. You need me. Besides," whined the crow, "it's all my fault. I feel so guilty, it's tearing at me inside. Let me make it up to you, kid."

"Look at the poor guy," said the buzzard. He blew a triple smoke ring this time. "Isn't he pitiful? A wreck, a walking shadow of a bird. Let him help you. Besides, you'll need it."

Billie hesitated. Clark Kent nudged her with his front bumper.

"Ahh, Billie. Can we talk?"

"Sure. Go on."

"Uh, just the two of us."

"I wouldn't dream of intruding," said the buzzard. "Besides, I have business of a personal nature with Dolores. Cairo will meet you by the door."

Once the two were out of earshot, Clark whispered urgently, "Billie, these birds are trouble. Stay away from them."

"I can't. How else can I find Bix?"

"Donuthole is a city full of Groupers. You'll be squished!" cried the reporter.

Cairo shouted over to Billie, "Come on, kid. Your little brother could be crying while you two are gabbing. He could be hanging upside-down in a cellar full of rats. And bats. And cockroaches. His nose could be running, with no one to wipe it for him."

"Okay," said Billie. "Let's go find him." She turned to Clark. "Will you come along? Please?"

"Impossible." The reporter was shaking again, his loose metal parts clanking together.

"You're not afraid of those Groupers, are you, Clark?" Billie asked.

"Of course not. I just don't want to go near them, that's all. Besides, I'm not allowed to risk my circuitry. Mommie would get cut off. Her screen would go blank. She'd plunge into an abyss of boredom."

"Mommie can read a book," snapped Billie. "This is important, Clark. My little brother needs me. And if you don't come, I'll be all alone with that crow."

Clark Kent fell silent a moment. His camera swiveled nervously from side to side. "It's against my better judgment. It's dangerous and stupid. Very stupid. But I can't let you go alone."

"I knew you would!" Billie kissed Clark Kent's watermelon head and sat herself in his wheelchair. She waved good-bye to Your Library Goat, who was in a literary discussion with a flock of finches. Outside the Bird Bar, the leather-capped crow hopped up into Billie's lap. The reporter revved into high-speed mode, and they rattled off down the road toward the city.

Far behind them, the albatross from the Bird Bar stood in the doorway, shaking one white wing furiously in the air. Cairo T. had left without paying for all those Strawberry Fizzes.

8

Snacks and Spectacles

Cairo T. Crow was an annoying traveling companion. He kept hopping nervously from Billie's lap to her head and back again, flapping his scraggly wings. Up close, he was a wreck. His worn leather cap was smeared with mud, and his red-rimmed eyes leaked an oozy yellow liquid, just like the hurt sparrow Billie and Mimi had once found in the park. He smelled like rancid strawberries.

"Step on it, Vidhead," the crow shouted. The roving reporter was already going so fast that the wind pressed Billie back into the wheelchair seat. The path ran smoothly through open country. They topped a hill.

In the valley below, the path was blocked by a forest of yellow blooms. Sunflowers. As Clark rolled closer, Billie realized the green stems were as tall and thick as trees. The flowers towered over her. Clark Kent stopped.

"Kent here. Live from a dead end." His video camera searched for an opening among the stems. "You're our guide, Cairo T. Where's the path?"

"Just get going!" ordered the crow.

"You said you could take us to Bix," said Billie worriedly. "Don't you know which way to go?"

"Not a clue, kid," the crow confessed. "But don't panic. Once we get to the big city, Cairo T. Crow knows every twist in the alley, every wrinkle in the flight path. The countryside is not my usual haunt."

"Uh-oh. We're lost," said Billie under her breath.

"Which way, Billie?" said Clark Kent.

"Cairo T. should know the way," fumed Billie. "It's *his* job."

"But Billie," protested Clark. "It's *your* brother. Turn back? Or into the sunflower forest? Choose."

Billie hesitated a moment. "Straight ahead!" she decided.

"Move it, Vidhead!" urged Cairo. "Get us through this endless flowerpot. I need another Fizz."

Clark edged his wheels between two huge stems, and made his way cautiously into the sunflower forest.

It was dark among the flowers, as their huge yellow heads blocked the sunlight from above. They could only creep along, and the farther in they went, the darker it became, and the narrower the spaces between the stems. Finally a pale green wall surrounded them on every side. Every direction seemed the same. There was nowhere left to go.

Trapped by giant sunflowers, Billie thought. I'll probably die right here. I'll starve to death in this crazy forest. I'll grow thin and pale and be forced to eat Clark's head for nourishment, and then I'll die anyway with a robot murder on my conscience. Mimi and Brian will be really sorry they made me go on tour, and asked me to take care of that brat Bix, and didn't let me go to school with real kids instead of having that idiot Pigbone blabber in my ear in fifty different cities. . . .

"Kent here. More lost than ever," the reporter muttered to himself.

"Clark," Billie said. "I'm sorry I got us into this mess. I thought it would be the best way to find Bixie, and now I don't know what to do. What do you think?"

"Think? I think Mommie will go nuts if all she keeps seeing are sunflower stems. Feeding Mommie live-action footage is the purpose of my existence, my reason to be! Filming a dark sunflower forest is not in my job description. I can't risk getting called in for repairs. I've made an awful lot of nature documentaries lately. She hates them. What if she puts me on kitchen duty? Even worse, what if she dismantles me?" The rambling reporter's camera began to swivel desperately, searching pointlessly for thrills among the stems. "Kent here. Still lost," he mumbled. "Action potential, nearly zero."

"Clark!" cried Billie, stomping her foot. "Can you forget about Mommie Darling for a minute? Bix is in serious trouble, and now we'll probably never find him." Billie was in tears. Clark turned toward her just as the first tiny drop rolled down her cheek. His camera stopped swiveling.

"Sorry, Billie. Even highly specialized journalistic equipment can get trapped in its own circuitry."

"That's okay, Clark," said Billie. "I just need you here with me. Cairo T. is totally worthless."

The crow was leaning against a sunflower stem in a Fizz-induced stupor. He began to snore. "Wake up, you dumb bird!" shouted Billie, walking over. She shook the crow by his scraggly shoulder. He squawked loudly in his sleep and fell over onto the grass. Carved into the sunflower stem, right where Cairo had been leaning, was a small sign. It looked like this:

Where it pointed, Billie could see a narrow path heading off into the darkness, just wide enough for the rambling reporter.

The three travelers soon found themselves with the sunflower forest at their backs and a rocky plain in front of them. On a nearby hillside stood a strangely constructed building that looked like a huge pair of eyeglasses. It seemed to be made of papier-mâché. A round door was built into one of the lenses. A large sign out front read:

THE ROVING EYE

Travelers Welcome
Snacks and Spectacles
CHANGE YOUR POINT OF VIEW

"Snacks!" shouted Billie. "I'm starving. Pull over, Clark." As the robot rolled to a stop next to one huge lens, the crow, who had been dozing fitfully in Billie's lap, squawked loudly and flapped his sooty wings.

"Pull out, Vidhead!"

"Stay right where you are, Clark" said Billie. "He's not our boss."

"Don't be stupid, girlie," cackled Cairo. "This place is on Archibald's guest list. He's Grouper numero uno. Anybody on his list is gonna be a permanent guest of the Kingfish. Trust me, kid. You don't want to be in that spectacle shop when the owners get a one-way ticket to Aqualand."

At this moment the round door of the cottage opened, and a small wiry raccoon lady in thick glasses and a leather apron appeared.

"Glasses or snacks?" she asked briskly, rubbing her paws together.

"Guest list or no guest list," said Billie, "I'm hungry."

"I'm with you, Billie," agreed Clark Kent. "Where the action is." The two of them headed for the open door.

"Numbskulls!" screamed Cairo. "Go ahead! I try to help you out, kid, and you don't listen to me. Get yourself in deep doo-doo! See if I care." And with that, the crow flapped his wings and glided up to a low branch of a nearby maple tree.

Inside the shop, tall shelves were overflowing with tools, old eyeglass frames, and other odds and ends. There was a long counter made of green glass, where rows of spectacles were laid out for inspection. Another raccoon in a yellow cap was working at a lens-grinding wheel. The lady raccoon set a cup of juice on the counter, along with a Marshmallow Fluff sandwich. "The specialty of the house," she said. "Hard to get these days. I'm Hilda, and that rude fellow in the corner is Morris."

"I'm Billie, and this is Clark Kent. Don't mind him. He's looking for action."

Clark had begun to swivel his camera around the shop. "Kent here. Live from the Roving Eye. Two affable raccoons run this spectacle and snack shop in—"

Suddenly Morris leaped from his workbench, a black cloth bag in one paw. Before the rambling reporter had a chance to object, Morris had slipped the bag over Clark's camera and his watermelon head. The raccoon tied it firmly with a piece of string.

"Help!" squeaked Clark. "I'm blind! Let me out of here! You don't understand! Mommie's screen is blank!!!" Clark rolled frantically into a wall, denting his front fender. "Mommie will be bored! She'll . . . she'll . . . I don't know what!"

"Damn them," mumbled Morris, "sending their contraptions around to spy on us." He turned toward Billie. "What's your dirty job? Writing up the reports?"

"Leave her alone, Morris," intervened Hilda, slapping him lightly on the paw. "She's only a child."

"Child? Hmmph. She's human, isn't she? You are human, aren't you?"

"I guess so," Billie replied.

"Humans are arrogant, lazy, greedy, and stupid."

"I am not!" cried Billie.

"They think they're better than everyone else, and they're ugly besides."

"You've only seen two," Hilda reminded him. "And you know you like Myron."

"Well," grumbled Morris, "the Kingfish is everything I just said—and worse."

"Don't get worked up, Morris," said Hilda. "She's a stranger in the Borderland. She can't hurt us." Morris relented, still twitching in anger.

"Don't worry about your friend," said Hilda as Billie ate her sandwich. "We'll take his blindfold off when you leave." Clark Kent stood quietly in the corner, fearful of banging into a table again if he tried to move. "We're sorry to blind him," continued Hilda, "especially since our business is giving customers a chance to see the world in many different ways. The Kingfish likes everyone to see it only one way: his way. We have to be careful."

Somewhere else in the universe, an enormous pile of bedclothes stirred. A white sea of sheets shifted, and the half-eaten cupcakes, the empty bags of jalapeño potato chips, the tubs of chocolate frosting, the bottles of taco sauce, the tangles of electric cable, the micro-tools, the circuit boards, the soldering guns, all rolled into new positions as Mommie Darling sat up. Her nightgown was smeared with chocolate and dusted with graham cracker crumbs. She was fat, but not terribly fat, and her wild curly hair framed a pleasant middle-aged face. Her voice pierced the silence of the bedroom. "Fixit! Fixit!"

The large metal spider immediately lowered from the ceiling. It headed toward Mommie's giant bed. "Fixit here. What's broken?"

"My screen's gone blank. Check all systems on Clark. Either he's wandered into a closet, or I'm calling him in for major repairs."

"Hang on while I run the diagnostic on our reporter." Lights flickered over a bank of switches in a far corner of the room.

"Clark is ship-shape, Mommie," called the chef and handyman. "That darkness on your screen is what he's transmitting. My advice?"

"I didn't ask for your—"

"Wait it out."

"Enough!" shouted Mommie, and Fixit retreated up into the rafters.

Mommie turned again to the screen. "Action!" she cried, but the screen stayed dark. "Clark, I'm gonna demote you to kitchen duty. You'll be scrubbing out cake pans. You'll be . . ." Mommie grew tired of threatening Clark. He couldn't hear her anyway. "Fixit! How about whipping up that famous marshmallow cake of yours?"

"I can't," called Fixit from the attic. "We're all out of marshmallows!"

Mommie sighed. No action, no marshmallows, no decent company.

Back at the Roving Eye, Billie told Hilda all about her Uncle Myron and Bix, while the raccoon climbed adeptly up and down the tall shelves, putting away spare eyeglasses. The raccoons knew Myron, and had even heard rumors about a creature called Bix arriving in the Borderland. They hadn't even known he was a human.

"Out here, we don't get much news, Billie," explained Hilda. "Most folks are afraid to visit us. This shop wouldn't pass official inspection. We make forbidden products. Have a look."

Billie looked over the row of spectacles displayed in the green glass case. Each had a card describing its function. The first pair for sale were ROSE COLORED. SEE THE WORLD, proclaimed the card, AS YOU'VE ALWAYS WANTED IT TO BE.

"Those can be dangerous," explained Hilda. "Morris ground the lenses out of a rare pink glass. They make for a lovely afternoon, but they can also be addictive. It can be very unpleasant to see the sadness and ugliness of the real world after you've seen it through our rose-colored glasses. I'd let you try them on, but they're dangerous for children."

Next were a set of blinders, like horses wear when they pull carriages. FOCUS ON THE PATH AHEAD, read the sign, AND IGNORE ANYTHING YOU DON'T LIKE. Alongside these were a pair of mirrored glasses, the card reading: PEOPLE LOOK AT YOU AND SEE THEMSELVES. Three pairs of glasses were labeled DISTANCE VISION: ONE MILE, TEN MILES, and ONE HUNDRED MILES. Another three read MICRO VISION: MOLECULAR, ATOMIC, and SUBATOMIC. One pair of glasses looked familiar. They were plain, dark lenses in a heavy silver frame. The sign below them merely read SHADES (CASE INCLUDED).

Billie pulled the glasses Uncle Myron had given her out of her jeans pocket. They were identical to the shades on display.

"Look at these," Billie said.

The raccoons both scrambled to see them, Hilda dropping down to the floor from a high shelf where she'd been putting away some equipment. Their little black noses twitched over Billie's hand. "Mine are just sunglasses," she said. "I've worn them a million times. They don't do anything special."

"Not where you come from," said Morris. "But I'd recognize my own handiwork anywhere. I sold these to your Uncle Myron a couple years ago. They're only made to work here in the Borderland. Try them on!"

Billie did. Everything seemed to blur for a moment, and then, somehow, she was looking into her old hotel room. "I don't believe it," whispered Billie, "there's the Pigbone." And there he was, trying on a paisley bathing suit in front of the mirror. "Can he see me?" she asked. Hilda's voice sounded as if it were coming from a great distance. "No, and he can't hear you either." The Pigbone danced a little jig and began stuffing argyle socks into a suitcase. He seemed happier than Billie had ever seen him. *"Bienvenue à Bermuda!"* he cried, disappearing into the bathroom. He emerged wearing a Hawaiian shirt and sandals, then he grabbed the suitcase and left. The hotel room was empty.

Billie wanted to follow the Pigbone down the hallway, to see Mimi and Brian, but she couldn't move. "Let me see my mom and dad, Hilda. Please!" The scene remained the same—the empty room, twilight outside the window. "Where are they?" Billie cried.

Morris's gentle paws lifted the glasses off. All around her, the Roving Eye reappeared. "Those glasses always see the place their case is located," said Hilda softly. "You have a case for these, don't you?"

"Yes." Billie sniffed. "A silver one. I couldn't find it when I packed. I must have left it somewhere in the Pigbone's room."

"That's the only place they'll let you see, then," explained Morris.

"Uncle Myron never told me," Billie said.

"Maybe," said Hilda, "he was going to tell you when you were older. Maybe he was going to bring you here himself someday."

Suddenly Morris put a paw to his lips. In the silence, Billie could hear a distant roar of engines. The Groupers.

"Morris," said Hilda, "the tunnel."

Morris nodded, and whipped the black hood off Clark Kent. "You can't let the Groupers find you here!" At the mention of Groupers, Clark's parts began a symphony of rattling and shaking. Hilda pulled aside a wall hanging to reveal a low door. "Head down, Billie. It's made for smaller animals than humans." The sound of approaching motorcycles grew louder. Billie and Clark ducked through the doorway, and Hilda called after them: "The tunnel leads to the hilltop. Good luck. We'll follow you in a minute! There are certain things we can't leave behind. Morris! Hurry up with those bags!" She slammed the door.

Billie and Clark were in total darkness. Suddenly, a beam of light lit the curved dirt walls of the tunnel.

"My headlight," explained Clark. "At least we won't dent ourselves crashing into rocks before the Groupers squish us to death."

"Don't talk like that, Clark," whispered Billie urgently. "You're a hard-nosed reporter. No emotions, remember?" She started running through the tunnel. The insurance medallion necklace bounced against her chest. Clark Kent raced bumpily along behind her, talking reassuringly to himself. "Kent here. Live from a tunnel. Action in progress. The bold reporter leads the way, bringing the frightened child to safety." They rushed on, Clark's headlight jiggling wildly. Where were Morris and Hilda? Had they gotten out in time?

The Groupers surrounded the Roving Eye, motorcycles idling. Their leader, Archibald, revved his engine. Tied to his saddle were Hilda and Morris, their paws lashed together with heavy rope. They hung off the motorcycle like two bedraggled balls of brown fur. Stuck to Archibald's helmet with masking tape were the rose-colored glasses. He had stolen them. Under his fin he carried a large jar of Marshmallow Fluff. He gurgled at his troops. "The human kid isn't here. Torch the place, Luther!"

"Right, boss! Spawned to Be Wild!"

"Just shut up and burn it down, Luther."

Up on the hilltop, hidden among the trees near the tunnel exit, Billie shuddered. "Looks like you're at the top of the guest list, kid," squawked Cairo T. Crow, fluttering down from a tree. "Archibald's Grouper numero uno. The Kingfish would never send him out for a couple of cut-rate raccoons."

Down below, Luther slid wetly off his motorcycle, wobbled over to one giant papier-mâché lens, and struck a match. In a moment, the Roving Eye was a mass of smoke and flame. The Groupers roared off with their prisoners. "Hatched to Ride!"

9

Bixopolis

Clark Kent rode all night. As the sun rose, he emerged from the woods onto an open hillside. His video eye swiveled over the wide plain below as the morning sun lit it bright orange. Billie awoke from where she'd fallen asleep in the robot's chair and stretched. The crow still dozed, perched on the reporter's watermelon head.

Billie got up and stepped to the edge of the hill. Below them, in the center of the plain, sprawled a large city. Neon lights glowed in the distance.

"Bixopolis," croaked the sleepy-eyed crow, who fluttered down onto her shoulder. "Home of your little brother Bix—glorious Bixopolis."

Billie's mouth dropped open. "BIXOPOLIS! Are you crazy? That entire place is named after my dorky two-year-old brother? He can't even talk right! Someone named a *city* after him?"

"Not *someone*," Cairo replied. His voice was like sandpaper on metal. "The Kingfish. That city was called Donuthole until yesterday. The Kingfish renamed it, after his new partner. Your brother. That boy among boys!"

"Partner?" echoed Billie. "But Bix is just a whiny baby! How can he be a partner? He doesn't even know how to share yet."

"Rumor says," explained the crow, "the Kingfish likes human company."

"Then this Kingfish is human, too?" asked Billie.

"Uh, not exactly," whispered the crow. He hopped back up onto Clark Kent's chair. "To Bixopolis, you hunk of junk. The town that never sleeps."

Bixopolis was a city of signs. Lights flickered around huge billboards, brilliant red neon flashing on and off.

HAVE MORE FUN—DRINK MORE FIZZ

Television screens cast a blue light out of all the shop windows. Each screen carried the same message:

Rule #11: PRIVATE PUDDING IS A CRIME
Rule #12: MARSHMALLOWS, TOO

Tattered posters were plastered on every inch of wall space:

MY MUSIC IS YOUR MUSIC
I KNOW WHAT'S GOOD FOR YOU

"What is this all about?" said Billie to herself. "Is it a joke?" The streets in the city were bumpy, so it was easier for her to walk than to ride Clark Kent, who occasionally had trouble negotiating a pothole. A family of scrawny rabbits hurried by them, the mother dragging one little girl by her furry ear. Another kid held a large marshmallow in his paw.

"Forbidden flavors!" screeched Cairo T. Crow, flapping his wings and hopping after them. "Regulation foods only!" With a sudden leap, he tore the marshmallow away with one yellow claw. "You bunnies know the rules! I'll turn this in at the palace. Now get lost." The rabbits scurried quickly around a corner and out of sight. Once they were gone, the crow popped the marshmallow into his beak and swallowed it. "Mmmm, marshmallow. No sense wasting this kind of tidbit on a bunny." He looked up at Clark Kent. "What are you staring at, Vidhead?" He hopped onto the rambling reporter again. "Let's get moving. We got a kid to find."

They rolled on through the streets of Bixopolis. Billie spotted a shabby flamingo leaning against a wall, a bottle of Strawberry Fizz at its feet. Stores were boarded up, and the streets were filled with a spooky silence. Standing in front of a small French bistro, Billie thought she recognized the duck she had met on the

Showboat. He was wearing an apron and hanging a new sign. The old one lay on the ground at his orange feet. DONUTHOLE BISTRO was being changed to BISTRO BIXOPOLIS. Billie waved to the duck, but he just quacked under his breath and went inside.

Printed pamphlets littered the streets, blowing in the morning breeze. Billie picked one up. On the cover was a picture of a narrow-faced man, about forty years old. His hair was slicked back and shiny, and he sported heavy sideburns. He was shown from the waist up, wearing a ruffled tuxedo shirt. Beneath the picture ran a caption: "He knows what's good for you." Inside the pamphlet, Billie found advertisements for Strawberry Fizz and recordings by a group called the Aqualand Glee Club. The cover picture was also offered for sale. "Buy one today! Let the Evolved Beauty of the King-fish inspire you and your loved ones!"

Cairo T. Crow fluttered overhead, calling out directions. "Make a left here," he squawked. Billie and Clark turned and found themselves in a small city square. The entire wall of the building facing them was covered by a giant poster:

VIVA BIXOPOLIS!

GRAND PARADE SATURDAY

MEET BIX, THE WONDERBOY

A hedgehog wandered into the square. He was dressed in denim overalls and yellow construction boots, with a guitar slung over one shoulder. With some difficulty he clambered atop a wooden crate. Gently, he strummed a few chords as a flock of starlings landed on a nearby rooftop to listen. A pair of young foxes, along with a group of strange fat lizards, scurried into the square. An elderly chimpanzee appeared in a doorway in her bathrobe, and a variety of other creatures leaned out of windows.

"Come on," cackled the crow, pulling on Billie's T-shirt with his beak. "Let's get moving."

"Wait just a second," Billie said, brushing him away. "I'm curious."

Just as the hedgehog was about to sing, a troupe of forty young girl animals in white satin jumpsuits ran helter-skelter into the square. Their costumes were decorated all over with purple and yellow spangles. There was an ostrich, the long skinny legs of her jumpsuit flapping in the breeze. There were a number of young kangaroos, and some striped monkeys. On the back of each uniform was written AQUALAND GLEE CLUB.

They stood with their arms around one another in the center of the square and began to sing.

A fish is a fish
Be he haddock or skate
A human is woman or man!
Some might not wish
For them all to relate—
But the Kingfish has a new plan!

The smallest singer, a mole who wore only a spangle around her tiny neck, leaped into the air like a high-school cheerleader and squeaked out her solo:

Kingfish, I'm your biggest fan!
Kingfish, I'm your biggest fan!

After all the dark rumors she'd heard about the Kingfish, Billie was surprised to hear his praises sung by these happy creatures. Could there be something good about him after all?

The Aqualand Glee Club sang on:

He knows about Fluff
He knows about taste
He's brought evolution to a whole new place!
He knows about pudding
He knows about songs
Kingfish knows about rights and wrongs!

Kingfish, I'm your biggest fan!
Kingfish, I'm your biggest fan!

"Sing, Woody!" shouted one of the foxes over the din of the glee club. On hearing the fox call out his name, the hedgehog in yellow boots perked up. He had stayed on his wooden crate the whole time, guitar ready.

"Woody! We're listening to you!" called some starlings from the roof. At that, Woody raised his arm high, stuck his wet black nose triumphantly in the air, and brought his paw down across the strings in a resounding chord. The glee club was still singing and swaying, but Woody's voice rang out loud and clear across the square.

Tonight the sharks of freedom will bite
Whoever tastes right, oh yeah
They're in the mood for Grouper stew
Sounds good to me too, oh yeah

Big fish in a small pond
Turn that fish eye
On yourself
Big fish in a small pond
You ain't no whale
You're sure to fail.

"Let's get out of here," said Cairo. "That idiot is singing 'Sharks of Freedom.' I hate that song."

"Nonsense," said Billie. "I want to see what happens."

"So do I," said Clark, zooming in on the guitarist. "Mommie will positively love this."

"I don't care what Mommie loves," complained the crow. "That hedgehog is Woody himself, and there's sure to be trouble." But Billie had stopped paying attention to the crow because she was listening to Woody's song. She could tell the singer really meant the words.

> *Tonight the sharks of freedom will eat*
> *A new kind of meat, oh yeah*
> *Feeding on leaders who strut and pose*
> *In satin clothes, oh yeah*
>
> *Big fish in a small pond*
> *Turn that fish eye*
> *On yourself!*

As Woody sang, the glee club sang even louder, trying to recapture their audience. "Kingfish, I'm your biggest fan!"

Woody kept singing, his face turned up to the sky.

Suddenly, a squadron of Groupers, scales glinting in

the sun, zoomed into the square on their motorcycles. The glee club members squealed and ran off, holding hands. Billie, followed by Cairo and Clark, ducked quickly behind an overflowing Dumpster. The smell was horrible, but they were safely out of sight.

Out in the square, Woody stood quietly on his box. The chrome choppers pulled up in front of him. The Groupers' sharp teeth gleamed from behind their flaccid, fishy lips. They slid off their motorcycles and held themselves upright on their fins.

Sitting comfortably in a sidecar, his molting head wrapped in a white silk scarf, was Bernard Buzzard. He nodded graciously to Woody as he climbed out. "*Enchanté*, my naughty hedgehog." He stomped to the center of the square, scattering a few gray feathers. When he reached Woody, who stood his ground, the buzzard leaned a heavy wing on the hedgehog's shoulder.

Archibald followed Bernard. The Grouper towered over Woody, dripping a fishy liquid down the back of the hedgehog's overalls. His henchfish stood menacingly by their choppers.

"Woody," oozed the buzzard, "I'm so sorry to see this happen. After our last little talk I felt sure you'd remember the rules." He looked out at the crowd that had gathered to hear Woody sing. "Doesn't it break your hearts to see a fellow creature so misled and confused? The Kingfish wants the best for everyone, Woody. He wants you to have a relaxing beverage to calm you down. All this excitement isn't good for you. Why don't I take you to the Aqualand Palace for a Strawberry Fizz?"

Archibald rested a heavy fin on Woody's neck. "Let me go!" the hedgehog screamed.

Bernard Buzzard looked out at the crowd again. "Don't you feel sorry for him?" he asked. "Resisting just the thing that'll make him feel better. Woody, I'm glad I got here in time. You're having some kind of breakdown."

"Even if I am," shouted Woody, "you can't arrest me for that!"

The voice of Archibald hissed and burbled through the water helmet that covered his head and gills. "You sang bad things about the Kingfish. Bad and unflattering things. You know he hates that. And what he hates, I hate." He moved even closer to Woody, his teeth showing.

"I hate it, too!" cried a voice from the Groupers.

"Shut up, Luther," rumbled Archibald.

"Don't look now," said Woody, "but your water helmet's got a leak." Archibald panicked, slapping at his helmet with both fins. He was fooled just long enough. Woody leaped off the crate and ran for it. But Luther was surprisingly quick, flopping forward to catch the hedgehog in the chest with a fin, knocking him to the ground.

"Now, boys," interrupted the buzzard, opening his wings wide to command attention. "We don't want any nastiness here. Woody, my fishy friends are getting upset. Be reasonable. You're only a furry mammal, a creature of swamp and woodland. How could *you* know more about how to take care of everyone than the Kingfish? He's a Professor of City Planning. He's the author of the entire *Encyclopedia of Important Knowledge*. Where he comes from, my little furry friend, he's been Emperor of the United Nations. The Kingfish has plans for us. Big plans."

"All lies!" shouted Woody, standing up again. He began to sing, louder than ever.

> *Tonight the sharks of freedom will bite*
> *Whoever tastes right . . .*

"Grab him," barked the buzzard. Archibald scooped the hedgehog up under one smelly fin. "Woody, I'm sorry it's come to this." The buzzard turned to face the crowd. "He'll be well-treated, I assure you all."

"I'm not going anywhere!" screamed the hedgehog as Archibald strapped him to the handlebars of Luther's chopper. "I'm not going!" Bernard Buzzard climbed back into his sidecar. In a cloud of dust, the entire squadron disappeared.

A hush descended on the square. Billie, Cairo, and Clark Kent emerged from behind the Dumpster. Billie was furious. "Cairo," she said, her voice rising, "that sleazy goon was your friend, Bernard Buzzard. He works with those Groupers. He's the one who said you'd help me find Bix. I can't believe I trusted you guys."

"*Bernard* Buzzard?" squawked the crow. "You've got it all wrong, kid. That was, uh, *Bosco* Buzzard. Bernard's twin brother. He's always been the black buzzard of the family."

"Don't lie to me," said Billie angrily.

"All right, kid. I'll tell you the truth. Bernard's got a problem. You ever hear of a split personality? Mondays he's Dr. Jekyll. Tuesdays he's Mr. Hyde. You ever read that book, Billie? It was my ex-wife's favorite. She was an actress—"

"Don't change the subject," snapped Billie. "And don't keep telling me these ridiculous stories. I want the truth."

"Don't even bother, Billie," said Clark Kent. "This crow just piles lies on lies. I always thought he was bad news. Hop on my seat. We can rescue Bix by ourselves."

The crow laughed a nasty cackling laugh. "Crazy

hunk of junk. Like I told you, the Aqualand Palace is crawling with Groupers. You'll never get past them without me. Even if you do, the place is a crazy maze inside. You'll wander in circles forever and never find Bix. And even if you do find Bix, you'll never make it out again—unsquished." The crow paused. "Go on," he croaked softly. "Go without me."

Billie hesitated. "All right, Cairo," she said. "Show us the way." What else could she do? The crow was her only hope.

10

Aqualand Palace

They made their way through narrow streets, leaflets underfoot and tattered posters peeling from the walls. At last they turned a corner and, with a quick flurry of feathers, the crow ducked behind a group of trash cans. "This is it," he whispered. Clark Kent rolled to a halt as Billie crouched down beside Cairo. Above their heads towered a stone arch, weathered by long exposure to wind and rain. It was intricately carved with creatures of the sea: sharks, mermaids, seahorses. Atop the arch, a huge stone dolphin leapt. Its tail was broken off, and so was its nose. Beneath it was carved the word AQUALAND. Beyond the arch was a dome-shaped building with a heavy door. Its windows were shaped like portholes. A particularly fat Grouper sat in a guardhouse, idly spraying Windex onto his water helmet and rubbing it clean with a rag.

"Welcome to the palace," said the crow.

"That is no palace," snapped Billie. "A palace has towers, and a moat and a drawbridge. That is a shabby old aquarium."

"Shhhh!" hissed Cairo. "Who are you to say what the Kingfish's palace should look like? Keep your mouth shut and wait here." The crow fluttered over to the guardhouse and whispered a few words to the fat Grouper. He returned holding an old metal key in his beak.

With Clark Kent a few paces behind, Billie followed the crow through another alley, circling the aquarium. The bird ducked under a hedge and, pulling aside some prickly rosebushes with his beak, revealed a low door set in the wall. It looked as if it hadn't been used for years. He looked back at Billie over one feathered shoulder as he put the key in the lock. The heavy door slid open with a fishy squish. "Right this way, kid. Watch your feet. We'll get your little brother outta here." The crow disappeared into the darkness. Billie hesitated a moment. She patted her pocket to make sure her special sunglasses were still there. She felt stronger knowing this fragile link to home was still with her.

The aquarium was hazy and smelled like disinfectant. The crow moved ahead, leading them through winding passages lit only by the glow from fish tanks and illuminated signs: GIANT TORTOISES, FIDDLER CRABS, FIJI BLOWFISH, LIFE OF A POND.

Billie was walking next to Clark when suddenly a bright beam of light flooded the corridor. The roving reporter had switched on his headlight. "Kent here. Live from the Aqualand Palace. Action potential, high."

"No, no!" warned Billie. "The Groupers'll spot us! Turn that off!"

"Billie, I've got to deliver quality footage. I can't turn my light off during a hot story."

"Clark, they'll squish us both! Bixie'll be stuck here forever! Turn it off!" The beam of the headlight dimmed, then disappeared.

"Kent here. Live from the Aqualand Palace," said Clark softly. "Intrepid reporter plunges ahead in darkness!"

On they went, the crow leading the way with a series of hops, flapping his wings. There were clumps of pinkish white glop on the floor that he was trying to avoid without much success. Little bits of it were clinging to the feathers on the underside of his body. It had a sweet, familiar smell, and Clark Kent's wheels were covered with a sheer film of it.

"What is this disgusting stuff?" hissed Billie to the robot, wiping a big blob off her shoe.

The crow heard her. "Disgusting stuff? You smart-mouth kid. Taste it, why don't you?" he squawked, flapping toward her. "Go on!"

"Gross!" cried Billie, shaking the blob off her fingers. "I'm not tasting it, you dumb bird. You taste it!" The crow hopped over to a large pile of glop and, with uncharacteristic delicacy, slurped a little of it up in his beak. "Mmmmm. Not bad. Not bad at all." Curious, Billie stuck her tongue out to lick her sticky finger. There was no mistaking it—vanilla pudding, Bixie's favorite food.

As she followed the flapping crow, Billie realized that all the aquarium tanks they'd seen so far had been empty, their fishy inhabitants long departed. They turned a corner and a large brightly lit tank marked TROPIC SEAS loomed into view. This one was occupied.

In it was a large reindeer with white fur, clacking around on brittle hooves among the remains of an underwater scene. Bright pink coral in strange and beautiful shapes covered the tank floor. Parts of the reindeer's antlers were missing, as if they had been broken off in a fight. Billie walked up to the glass of the tank and stared. Clark Kent excitedly zoomed in.

"A reindeer!" he whispered. "Mommie Darling will go wild, Billie! Since the Kingfish arrived, they've all disappeared."

"Why?" asked Billie, trying at the same time to get the attention of the reindeer by waving her arms.

"Nobody knows."

"Maybe he knows something about Bixie." Billie knocked gently on the glass. "Excuse me! Excuse me! Mr. Reindeer!"

The reindeer looked up and answered in a deep, melodic voice, "Is someone speaking to me? It's hard to see out there in the dark."

"Do you know anything about a two-year-old human boy?" asked Billie.

"Go away," the reindeer said. "I have nothing to say to Groupers."

"Groupers?" cried Clark Kent. "Not us. I am a journalistic servo-mechanism, on the trail of a hot story. And she's . . . she's . . . Billie. She's not even from the Borderland."

"Sing!" commanded the reindeer.

"What?"

"Sing!" he repeated. "Groupers don't have music. If you do, I might talk to you."

Billie took a deep breath. She sang, in a soft, clear voice, the ballad that Mimi had made the finale of her world concert tour. It was her favorite of all her mother's songs.

Underneath the silver moon
Skating on thin ice
A crack beneath my unsure feet
And down into the deep
I go

The neon fish slide softly by me
As I look at the sky
They think I can't fly
But up into the night
I go

"Lovely, my deer." The reindeer's manner had changed. "I was a singer, too, you know. Before the Kingfish came." Here the reindeer bowed low to show Billie the broken stubs on his head.

"What happened to your antlers?" she asked.

"They are not antlers at all. They are horns. Here in the Borderland, all the reindeer made beautiful music together. We were a natural marching band, and the songs of our migration at the start of the long winter could be heard for miles as we traveled the country. But no longer. The Kingfish silences any music that doesn't praise him. The other reindeer all fled into the Endless Desert. No one knows what happened to them. I'd injured my foreleg playing soccer and couldn't travel, so I stayed behind. Early one morning the Groupers caught me trumpeting a sunrise song and—" Here the reindeer broke off suddenly. "Did you say something about a human boy?"

"His name is Bix. Do you know where I can find him?"

"I wouldn't, if I were you. He—"

"No fraternizing with the prisoners!" The crow had skittered back through the halls to find them. "Talkative reindeer will be tattled on!" He leaned toward Billie. "Stop wasting your time with that musical quadruped, kid. Bixie's close. The wonderboy is right around the corner."

"Good-bye, reindeer!" said Billie. The prisoner tapped one hoof nervously and didn't answer. Cairo grabbed her by the arm and pulled her at top speed down the hallway. He was unsteady, often banging his head against the glass wall of one of the tanks, or misnegotiating a leap and landing in puddles of sticky liquid. Clark Kent wheeled along behind him.

As they rushed along, Billie caught glimpses of other prisoners in their fish tanks. An obese hippopotamus, almost filling her enclosure, lolled under a sign reading HAMMERHEAD SHARK. Another tank was filled with tiny rodents, who scurried furiously up and down the walls. In a tank labeled ARCTIC WATERS were Hilda and Morris. The fluorescent light on the raccoons was intense.

Hilda lay curled up in a corner, one paw shielding her eyes. Rotten fruit and fish heads were scattered over the blue concrete floor. Morris paced the tank nervously. He looked thin, like a bag of bones under his matted brown fur. Billie wanted to do something to help them. She wanted to shout, to break the glass.

The crow grabbed her arm, jerking her forward. "We're almost there, kid." From somewhere, Billie could hear a creature singing softly.

> *Big fish in a small pond*
> *Turn that fish eye*
> *On yourself . . .*

Cairo dragged Billie around a corner. There, in the largest tank of all, the one built for a killer whale, lay her little brother. He was asleep in a white enamel bathtub. On its side, big gold letters read **BIX.**

Billie ran to the tank and pressed her nose against the glass. She could hear a voice, deep and insistent, from somewhere in the tank. It said the same words over and over—a recording. "I am the future. You are the future. I am your Kingfish. You are my son. I am the future. You are the future. I am your Kingfish. You are my son."

"Bix!" Billie shouted. "BIX!" But her brother dreamed on, that hypnotic voice surrounding him.

Suddenly, a sharp claw grasped her shoulder, and gray wings beat the air around her. She was lifted up off the ground, kicking and screaming.

"Clark, help me!" Billie twisted and struggled, but the sharp claws only dug deeper into her flesh. She was lifted high into the air. "Clark!"

Billie landed with a crash in a tank marked ELECTRIC EEL. The floor was covered with shiny blue gravel that cut her hands. At the open top of the tank she could see the molting head of Bernard Buzzard looking down at her. "*Enchanté*, Miss Billie," he cackled. Then he disappeared.

A prisoner. Those rotten birds had set her up after all. The crow had lured her to Bixie, and then they trapped her like a fish in a bowl.

"Ah! You beautiful birds!" A deep voice resonated through the long corridors. "You brought me the sister." Was that the same voice that was playing in Bix's tank? Billie strained to see its source, but she could only make out shadowy shapes through the glass. The voice continued. "My Groupers have been trying to squish her for days."

"Groupers couldn't squish her, boss," said the familiar croak of the crow. "Couldn't even find her. Cairo T. Crow brought her right to the palace. Just like I brought Bix."

"I don't plan to make her nearly as comfortable as her brother."

The elegant tones of the buzzard chimed in. "Shall we squish the young lady now—or squish her later?"

"Later. I'll have a chat with her in the morning. Tell Archibald." Here the new voice became extremely chummy. "And now a merit badge and a bag of marsh-mallows for you, Cairo. You've earned it."

As the crow squawked appreciatively, Billie thought she saw the dark outline of Clark Kent's head retreating into a corner. Someone else must have seen it, too. "What's that behind you?" cried the new voice, its tone changing abruptly. "You Fizz-soaked piece of poultry! How could you bring that machine in here? Don't you know what that melon-headed robot does? It videos everything! Bernard! Smash its lens in!"

"Kent here! Live from Aqualand!" screeched Clark Kent, his metallic voice rising in panic. "Your reporter boldly faced—"

Trapped in her tank, Billie cringed at the sound of splintering glass.

11

Teatime at Mommie's

"I told that crow the Cadillac was no good to him, that it would pitch him into the air like a bucking bronco, but he didn't care. He just cackled, 'Bet it anyway. It's all you got.'"

Uncle Myron, otherwise known as the Great Nostromo, was standing up on Mommie Darling's giant bed, pacing back and forth among the circuit boards and candy wrappers and waving his hands in the air. An afternoon tea party was in progress. Myron had brought a big box of mini-marshmallows from the other side, and Fixit had outdone himself in the kitchen: taco chips with marshmallow dip, marshmallow cake, Rice Krispie treats, and marshmallows flambé. Mommie and her guests were gorging themselves on the rare delicacies.

Fixit swung freely around the room, refilling cups. King Buster squatted on a pile of pillows, chomping a marshmallow. Madame Zanoni, wearing the ratty pink bathrobe that was her offstage attire, drank tea out of a huge bucket. Mommie herself balanced her teacup delicately on one knee. She had done her hair nicely for her visitors, though she was still in her nightgown. Myron continued, shouting at no one in particular.

"I told Cairo the car was made for human beings only. Its internal gizmos and gear-jammers connect only with the human sensorium. Only human legs can reach all the necessary pedals! Only human eyes can see all the important colors on the dashboard!" He turned to Mommie. "Cairo won't be able to handle it—will he?"

Mommie Darling grimaced. "Myron, you know I built that car ages ago, back when I did that sort of stupid thing. I've long since stopped wanting to go across the Endless Desert, and I'm sure I can't remember what the Cadillac will and won't do. You shouldn't have let it out of your hands. Gambling is a horrible habit. My ex-husband, Herman Mudhen—"

"Cairo cheated you, Myron," interrupted King Buster, his mouth full of marshmallow cake. "He always does. You shouldn't play cards with him anymore."

"You know what this means, don't you?" Myron said to Mommie Darling. "I won't be able to go back and forth between the worlds."

"Pity," said Mommie, with a little crease of a smile at

the side of her mouth. "You'll just have to join me for tea more often."

"Without the Caddy," Myron continued, "I'm trapped here forever."

"All the better," Mommie Darling reasoned. "I should never have given that car to you in the first place. The human world is nasty. Very nasty. After I took that strange ride in the Nevada desert where I collapsed, fell off the camel, and found myself at the Silver Moon Motel, I should have realized how lucky I was. I should have never built that car to carry me back. Stupid nostalgia. That world is not worth going back to. It was there, on the other side of the Endless Desert, that Herman Mudhen, that compulsive gambler and would-be ladies' man, dumped me. On our honeymoon. He even took the car. The little weasel didn't have the courage to look me in the eye. That man had a mean streak, Myron. He emptied our joint bank account. If I ever—"

"Mommie," interrupted Myron. "I know all about Herman Mudhen. You always tell me. Let's talk automobiles. You've got to build me another one."

"Sorry, Myron dearest. If I built you the car, you might go away and never visit me again."

"Did I ever stay away long when I *had* the car?" said Myron, a touch of pleading in his voice.

"*Much* too long," said Mommie, pouting. "Besides, you don't really care about me or you'd have introduced me to your niece."

"Billie? How can I possibly introduce you, Mommie Darling, if you refuse to leave the Borderland?"

"But you've brought her here."

"Certainly not!"

"But we saw her on screen! Didn't we, Fixit?"

"Yes indeed," affirmed the chef.

"I remembered her from the photos you brought with you after her birthday party last year," said Mommie. "Didn't you say that your sister Mimi is a rock star? She's probably making a mess of her children. My ex-husband, Herman Mudhen, used to dream of stardom, but he couldn't sing. He sounded like a bellowing hippo in chains. His only talents were for losing money and picking up showgirls. He was nothing but a weasel in a white leather jumpsuit."

Myron interrupted. "Mommie! This is important! When did you see Billie? Where was she?"

"Don't you know?"

"No," answered Myron nervously, "I don't."

"Well," explained Mommie, "Clark Kent filmed Billie a couple days ago talking to an old goat. Boy, was she boring. The goat, I mean. I turned off my screen. Later, my reporter went black for almost an hour. Transmission trouble. I didn't try him again until this afternoon, and now he's not broadcasting at all!"

"Think of it, Mommie!" cried Myron. "Billie, lost in this strange world, without anyone to help her. She must be—"

"Myron, wait." Mommie, her mouth full of taco chips, waved her hand at him. "Fixit said Clark's systems were still working when he went black yesterday. Maybe something was recorded this morning while I was busy with an important repair job. Fixit!" shouted Mommie Darling. "Rerun whatever Clark Kent shot this morning. Roll tape!"

The giant screen sprang to life, flashing images of the city as Clark Kent rolled through its streets.

"There she is!" Myron shouted. "That's Billie!"

"I didn't know they'd gone to Donuthole," said Mommie Darling. "I haven't been there in years. Have you, Myron?"

"No," answered Myron. "Not since the Kingfish took over. A year ago, his Groupers tried to arrest me."

"Arrest you? What for?"

"Doing my magic act for some kids. It seems the Kingfish insists on providing all the entertainment himself. Zanoni, Buster, and I escaped in the Cadillac.

We've worked on the Showboat ever since." Myron looked back at the video screen. "Donuthole doesn't look the way I remember it. The streets are dead."

A wall poster reading

I KNOW WHAT'S GOOD FOR YOU
—Your Kingfish

flashed on screen.

"Did you ever meet this Kingfish?" asked Mommie Darling.

"Never," said Myron. "I was too busy running from his Groupers."

"With just three of us humans who've slipped across," complained Mommie, "and him here a year now, you'd think he'd have the courtesy to come over and introduce himself to me."

"He clearly has other things to do," said Myron, staring unhappily at the sequence of threatening wall posters flashing across the screen. "From the looks of Donuthole, he's been making some horrible changes."

King Buster piped up. "I just remembered something, Myron. I met that human girl on the boat."

"You did?"

"Yes, we both did," Zanoni explained mildly. "But we didn't know she belonged to you, did we, Buster?"

Myron's brow clouded. "You saw a human child and you didn't tell me?"

"We got busy, remember?" croaked Buster, hopping into Madame Zanoni's lap for protection. "The Showboat sank! She was a sweet kid. Worried about her brother Nix."

"Bix?"

"Yeah. Bix. She was trying to find him."

"Then both of them are here!" exclaimed Myron. "This is terrible. Bix is just a baby! Brian and Mimi will be desperately worried. I'll have to send them a message telling them the kids are safe with me! Fixit! Can you handle that?"

"I can handle anything," the handyman said calmly from above.

"This is a disaster!" cried Myron. "I'm lying to my sister! I lost her kids!! I've lost my Cadillac!!!"

The rambling reporter's taped voice filled the room: "Kent here. Live from Bixopolis. Potential for action, medium to high."

"Bixopolis?" said King Buster. "Hey, Myron! The Kingfish renamed Donuthole after your nephew!"

"No, it can't be," said Myron. "Fixit, fast-forward! I need to know where they end up."

The video cut ahead to a scene in some dark corridor.

In front of the reporter's wavering camera, two figures moved.

"There's Billie again!" King Buster shouted. "And someone's with her."

The other figure was a bird with scraggly black feathers. Myron's face tightened in recognition. Cairo T. Crow. On screen, there was a sudden blur of flapping wings, a tilt and shudder of the camera, and Billie's voice yelling, "Clark, help me! Clark!" Crash of splintering glass and the harsh clang of metal on metal. Then silence, and the screen went black.

On the outskirts of what used to be known as Donuthole was the recently renamed Bixopolis Sanitary Engineering Landfill Project. A mountain of trash floating in a soggy swamp. The Kingfish's garbage dump.

On the edge of that trash mountain something stirred. The sun glinted on the cracked lens of a video camera, poking up from a pile of coffee grounds and rotten orange peels. Then, shedding old newspapers, fish bones, muck, and debris, the bent and smashed body of Clark Kent, rambling reporter, rose up out of the trash and shook itself like a wet dog. His wheelchair seat was gone, his camera was partly smashed, his melon head was cracked down the middle. But his wheels were still usable, though bent and out of alignment, and his circuits were still intact. Mommie had built her reporter to last.

With various pieces of garbage still clinging to his body, Clark managed to slide down the trash heap and onto the road. The going was slow, as one wheel was badly bent. Even with a rusted bedspring dragging behind him and spokes popping from one wheel, Clark's damaged camera kept swiveling, looking for the action that kept Mommie happy. At the same time, another part of his circuitry knew he was no longer transmitting. He was only searching out of electric habit. He had to get home for repairs. That's what Mommie had programmed him to do.

Clark rolled free of the last of the trash. He turned toward Mommie Darling's, his internal homing device still functioning. He was the only moving thing in a wide landscape of salmon-colored hills, dotted with glorious marigolds. They were Clark's favorite flower, but he didn't even notice them. He kept thinking, a feverish buzz and tumble in his circuitry.

"What is my true purpose?" he asked himself. "To feed action sequences to a lonely woman in a bed? To wander aimlessly, seeking cheap thrills? Or is there more to my life? Are even the most artistic of nature documentaries enough to make my existence worthwhile? And what about Billie? What happened to her back there in the aquarium? Is she still alive? If the Kingfish and his Groupers smashed me and threw me in a garbage dump, what would they do to Billie? And her little brother?"

A burst of electric habit from his main circuits reminded Clark he should be focused on getting home to Mommie for repairs.

"Who cares what Mommie wants!" said Clark to his own circuitry. The feedback loop he created set his driveboards smoking. "What about what *I* want? And what about Billie?"

In one decisive moment, with an electronic crackle and the harsh humming sound of programming circuits frying and melting, Clark Kent turned around and rolled back toward Bixopolis, away from Mommie Darling, away from repair and safety. He wanted to help Billie. She was in danger, and broken as he was, he'd do whatever he could to save her.

Clark Kent didn't get far. A familiar croaking voice interrupted his progress. "There's that hunka tin! There he is! Hey, you! Newsboy! Whoaaaa!" Clark halted, and in a moment, Madame Zanoni, shambling along as fast as she could, her pink bathrobe flapping around her, caught up to him. On her back was a man with a swirling mustache whom Clark recognized immediately as the Great Nostromo, Billie's Uncle Myron. On his shoulder was King Buster.

"Newsboy," croaked Buster. "You'd better get back to Mommie for repairs. You're heading the wrong way, you know! Something wrong with your programming?"

"I'm overriding it!" cried Clark. "I know I'm supposed to return immediately on malfunction, but I won't do it! I'm on a rescue mission!"

"Clark," coaxed Myron, sliding down off Madame Zanoni's back. "You're in no condition to go anywhere."

"I've been with Billie every step of the way," Clark told them. "I won't go home now! If my programming can't make me, you certainly can't!" With that, the reporter took off, as quickly as he could manage. His parts rattled, watermelon seeds dropped from his cracked head, and he swerved erratically.

"Wait!" called Myron, climbing back onto Madame Zanoni. Madame chased after Clark, gaining on him bit by bit. Just as she caught up to him, the roving reporter veered precariously, skidded across the road on his bent wheel, crashed into a tree, and collapsed in a heap. Steam poured out of his drive motor and little popping noises came from the wreckage of his video equipment. His melon head was smashed to pieces. A red button flashed on and off near what used to be his head: EMERGENCY AUTOPILOT TO MOMMIE.

Myron pressed the button. The battered wheelchair righted itself and began rolling slowly away from Bixopolis and toward Mommie Darling's home. There was no glimmer of Clark Kent's determined reporter personality. The remains of the watermelon head lay scattered behind him on the ground.

"It's better this way, I suppose," said Madame Zanoni.

"He'll get home safe, I think," Myron added. "And Mommie is a genius. She can fix him, I'm sure."

With that, he and King Buster climbed aboard the elephant. "Madame Zanoni, my darling," Myron said. "Here is where we show what we are made of. Here is where greatness and character shine. Speed is what we need, Madame. Do your best!"

Madame Zanoni grunted, wheezed, and then trumpeted loudly. She pushed herself into a steady, ground-covering elephant lope.

"Way to go, babe!" shouted King Buster as the trio headed for the gloomy towers of Bixopolis.

Audience with the Kingfish

Billie was thrown facedown on the greasy cement floor of the seal pond courtyard. Her chin ached from the impact and her stomach churned at the stink of raw fish and disinfectant. There was an oily shine on her wrist where Archibald had been twisting her arm. He stood nearby, breathing heavily into his water helmet.

Struggling onto her knees and shivering in the cool of the morning, Billie looked around her. The seal pond was in the very center of the old aquarium, under a dome. It was filled to the brim with a thick white glop—vanilla pudding. The island in the middle of the pond, where seals once sunned themselves, had been painted bright colors and sprinkled with confetti. Lights blinked on and off from atop each rocky peak: red, blue, and purple.

From behind the island emerged a man, waist deep in the heavy pudding. He was shirtless and wore a spangled white satin jacket with wide lapels. The bottom edge of it trailed in the pudding. The lines around his mouth were hard and cold.

"Rise, and bear witness to the future," he said calmly, wading toward Billie through the thick white glop. She recognized the voice she'd heard in the aquarium corridor the night before. "I am your Kingfish," he continued. "I know what's good for you."

"Indeed he does," wheezed a familiar voice from somewhere. "Rule One: Always Look Your Best in the Presence. Rule Two: Always Smile in the Presence. Rule Three: Don't Bring Your Troubles to the Kingfish, or He'll Bring Trouble to You."

It was a moment before Billie could locate the source of the soft voice. It was Your Library Goat! She was in a corner on the far side of the courtyard, chained to the floor with a spiked collar around her neck. Her old beaded sweater had been replaced by a spangled jacket. She didn't even seem to see Billie.

Billie sprang to her feet and headed toward the chained goat.

"Stay where you belong, if you know what's good for you!" burbled Archibald threateningly.

"How dare you!" thundered the Kingfish, throwing a

fistful of pudding at the Grouper. It splattered across Archibald's helmet. "I'm the one who knows what's good for her! Keep your tongue in your fish head, you fake amphibian. Go right ahead, Billie. Have a little chat with your friend."

Billie reached Your Library Goat and touched her gently on the shoulder. "Library! It's me, Billie!"

"Hello, dear," whispered the prisoner, her eyes focusing. The fur on her head was matted and greasy. Billie reached around the metal collar and tried to open it. "It's no use," Your Library Goat whispered. "The Kingfish has the only key. I've been chained up here for days. I recite official rules, and sing lullabies to the Kingfish at night. He has trouble sleeping."

"Kingfish," barked Billie, turning around and striding toward the pond. "You can't keep someone locked up like that. Look at her! If you don't let her out right now, I'll hit you in the nose! I'll burn all your ugly little pamphlets to cinders! I'll—"

Billie choked on her words as something heavy and powerful began to churn the pudding surface. The Kingfish smiled a sickening smile, and out of the pond, in huge, scaly orange coils, rose the thick humps of a serpent's tail. His tail. It thrashed up through the pudding, scattering lumps of it across the courtyard floor. Archibald stepped back a few feet and Your Library

Goat cringed closer to the wall. The tail, slowing to a halt, remained curving up out of the pudding in five huge loops that circled the island in the center of the pond. The very tip, still thicker than Billie's leg and covered with spiky fins, rested on the edge of the pool, tapping the extra pudding off itself impatiently.

Billie backed off in horror. Stumbling away, she felt herself bump up against Archibald. His fin closed around her wrist again. "Let go of me!" shouted Billie, twisting her body around and kicking the fish in his soft underbelly. The Grouper just held her tighter. She turned toward the Kingfish. "You're a monster!" she cried.

The Kingfish laughed. "'Monster' is not the name I'd choose for my particular brand of evolutionary achievement. In fact, the ideal name hasn't yet been invented. I am more than human. I am more than fish. I am much, much more than reptile. I have accomplished"—and here he rolled the curves of his tail majestically in and out of the pudding—"the ultimate leap in the natural world. I have evolved forward, backward, up and over the reaches of the imagination. A kind of fourth-dimensional adaptation. Survival of the fittest, Billie. That's how it all works. They taught you that in school, didn't they? Didn't they?"

"I don't go to school," Billie answered. "I have a tutor."

"Survival of the fittest. Who thought of that one, Billie?"

"Darwin."

"That feeble theoretician. I practice what he only preached. Who is more fit than I? I swim, I breathe, I squeeze, I talk, I roil and coil and tie myself in knots. I bench-press two hundred pounds. I am the best rule maker, the best city planner. I know what's good for all creatures, great and small. My trans-species state is a step beyond. Two steps beyond, Billie. Darwin said it."

Billie knew this wasn't what Darwin said at all, but she had more important things on her mind. "Where's my little brother, you monster?" she cried, interrupting him. "Hand him over! He's just a baby. What do you want? Money from my parents or something?"

"Don't get so excited," replied the Kingfish. He began polishing one of the shiny orange loops of his tail with a handkerchief. "It's a sick demand for attention. Doesn't your mother take care of you properly?"

"Let me see Bix, you psycho!" yelled Billie. "And tell your goon to get his oily fins off me!"

"Relax." The Kingfish smiled. "I know what's good for you. You must be thirsty. Have a Strawberry Fizz, and we'll bring Bixie out for a visit. It's time for his feeding, anyway. But first I'd like to educate you. I'm not sure you understand the way things work around here. You don't yet know what happens when people break the rules. LUTHER!"

Luther appeared in the entranceway and waddled obsequiously toward them, trundling a fish tank on wheels. He rolled it over to the edge of the pond. Inside, crouched in a corner with a big rock tied to his waist, was Woody. He looked hungry and dejected, and someone had taken away his guitar.

The Kingfish tapped on the glass. "Woody, wake up!"

The hedgehog roused himself and looked out angrily. "I am awake, Kingfish!" he cried. "I'm awake and I can sing without my guitar! I'll sing so loud you'll hear me in your dreams. I'll sing so loud you won't ever get to sleep!"

"Luther, give this irritating mammal a bath."

Luther pressed a big button on the side of the tank. It began to fill with water. Woody's eyes widened in terror. When the water reached his waist, he flailed his paws in a desperate attempt to swim, but the rock kept him stuck to the floor.

"Stop!" Billie cried, trying to wrench herself free from Archibald's grasp. "You'll kill him!"

The water stopped rising just when Woody's nose

was the only part of him still above it. The hedgehog, head tilted back, was breathing in and out frantically, struggling to keep his nostrils from filling up. The Kingfish chuckled. "Hedgehogs can't swim anyway, you know. They're an evolutionary dead end. The rock just makes their struggle more amusing. I haven't tied a rock to you yet, Billie. Luther! Take this puny rodent away. Bring Bix, my Wonderboy!" Luther hit the button again and the water rushed out of the fish tank and onto the floor. It splashed over Billie's toes. Luther wheeled Woody away.

"Billie," asked the Kingfish, "do you find me handsome?"

"No," she answered. "In fact, you're the ugliest, nastiest person I ever met."

"Rule Number Five!" quavered Your Library Goat from the corner. "If you can't say anything nice, keep your mouth shut or you'll be squished."

"It's been a year since I've been to the other side of the Endless Desert," the Kingfish continued. "That's a very long time. When I fell out of that human world of yours one sleepless night, quite by accident, I still walked on two legs, just like you. I was a successful man: Secretary Admiral at the United Nations, the respected author of an *Encyclopedia of World Knowledge*, complete in one volume, and an ex–National Football League linebacker. I thought being a mammal was just as great as it gets.

"Until I came to the Borderland, I didn't see the truth. Once I got here, my latent genius began to surface. My body began to alter, responding to the superior impulses of my brain. First I grew scales; then bit by bit I left my species behind. I am the stuff of legends. You've heard of mermaids and mermen, haven't you, Billie?"

"Yes."

"I am more than just a merman, because I don't have a mere fish tail. I have the tail of the sea serpent, lord of the briny deep." He paused. "As I said, I've been in the Borderland a long time. Styles may have changed elsewhere, and a leader needs to look up-to-date. Does your father wear sideburns, Billie?"

"What does it matter to you?"

"Surely you understand me. It's a fashion question." The Kingfish smoothed his greasy hair with one pudding-slick hand. "Even a legend needs to look his best."

Luther returned, pushing the white enamel bathtub with the golden letters **BIX** on its side. In the tub, waist-deep in pudding, sat the Wonderboy himself. Bix had grown tremendously fat. His cheeks were fleshy pink blobs. On his chubby nose were the rose-colored glasses Billie saw Archibald steal from the Roving Eye. He looked glazed, like someone who has just eaten a huge meal.

"Bixie!" cried Billie. Archibald let go of her arm and she ran over to her brother. "Bixie! Are you okay?" She gave him a big kiss. Sluggish as he was, Bix smiled at her.

"Billixa. Morpho podnucker." He clapped his sticky hands together, starting to look interested.

The Kingfish interrupted. "Wonderboy," he cooed, extending his long scaly body over the edge of the pond until he hovered right above Bix's tub. "Wonderboy, who loves you?"

"Fishy," answered Bix, putting a handful of pudding in his mouth.

"Who knows what's good for you?"

"Fishy."

"Your mom and pop never loved you like I do, Bixie. If they really care, why don't they come looking for you? They don't give a damn, that's why. They've already forgotten all about you. I let you play with matches and have all the pudding you can eat. That proves we belong together." The Kingfish lowered his voice, his face inches from Bix's ear. He whispered hypnotically: "I am the future. You are the future. I am your Kingfish. You are my son."

The Kingfish turned abruptly to Billie. "Get in the tub."

"It's full of slimy pudding," she cried. "No way."

"Rule Number Forty-eight!" called Your Library Goat from the corner. "Never say 'No way'!"

"It's good for you," continued the Kingfish, raising a hand to silence Library. "It'll calm you down. Nice, cool pudding. Not everyone around here is allowed to have pudding, did you know that? Now get in or Luther will help you in."

"Yeah," piped up Luther. "I'll help ya with this!" He curled a heavy fin into a fist and shook it at Billie.

"Shut your gills, Luther!" barked the Kingfish. "Now get in the tub." Gingerly, Billie stepped in next to her brother. The pudding slopped into her sneakers with a sloshing sound. She sat down. It felt weird, like a thick bath of snot. Bix goggled at her through his rose-colored glasses and played with her hair.

"Bixie," she whispered, "I'll get you out of here, I promise!"

"No private conversations!" thundered the Kingfish. "I won't tolerate whispering of any kind." His chin rested on the edge of the bathtub and Billie could see the flecks of food between his teeth. "Billie, you are proving to be a troublemaker." He lashed his tail up and down, spattering pudding across the courtyard. "I can have you squished at any moment. Do you realize that?"

"Then why don't you?"

"Wonderboy's training isn't yet complete," answered the Kingfish. "Soon he will love only me. But at the moment, he's still slightly fond of you. I don't want to upset him before the Grand Parade tomorrow. I'm officially introducing him to the citizens of Bixopolis." Here the Kingfish tousled Billie's hair with a pasty hand. "Besides, you'll learn to love me, too. I'm very charming when I want to be."

"I'll never learn to love you!" snapped Billie, and threw a handful of pudding right into the Kingfish's eyes. The Kingfish reared back in fury, the giant orange tail coiling and thrashing.

"SQUISH HER, ARCHIBALD! SQUISH HER NOW!"

As Archibald lurched forward, Bix woke out of his stupor. "Billixa podrucker!" he shouted excitedly. "Billixa podrucker!"

"No, Bixie!" answered the Kingfish. "That's impossible."

"Podrucker fulco!" cried Bix. "Fishy fishy!"

"HOLD IT, ARCHIBALD!" shouted the Kingfish.

The Grouper stopped his advance. He flashed his rows of teeth at Billie. "Some other time," he burbled.

"Bix wants you to be in the Grand Parade," said the Kingfish angrily, wiping the pudding off his face.

"Billixa!" cheered Bix.

"I won't make any trouble, I promise." Billie managed a strained smile. "Please. Let me be in the parade with my little brother."

"Perhaps," said the Kingfish. "LUTHER! Take them away! And have yourself a marshmallow from storage bin ten. You deserve it."

It was the familiar Princess Suite. The walls were bare. Where were the maps and charts? Where were the stacks of books she used for her lessons? Where was the Pigbone? Billie looked around frantically. The beds were made crisply, hotel-style, and the bathroom was full of fluffy white towels. Where was everyone?

The door began to open and Billie heaved a sigh of relief. It was Brian or Mimi. It had to be! They wouldn't leave Omaha without her! But it was only Mr. Eggwater, the headwaiter from room service, wearing his spiffy dark uniform and wheeling a silver cart.

"Mr. Eggwater!" Billie yelled at the top of her lungs. "Mr. Eggwater, where are my mom and dad?" She was shouting, but Mr. Eggwater couldn't hear her. He was busy stocking a tiny refrigerator with mineral water and wine. "Mr. Eggwater!" Billie was frantic. Where were her parents? How could they go off somewhere and not even leave a note?

"Prisoner!" thundered a burbly voice. Billie remembered where she really was. She tore off the sunglasses Uncle Myron had given her and found herself still in the empty fish tank. Archibald leaned over the front glass, looking down on her through the water bubbling in his helmet.

"Yes?" she answered weakly.

"Turn over the glasses."

"No way!" she cried, clutching them tightly in her fist. "They're private property."

"Nothing's private here. Not for you. Especially sunglasses. The Kingfish wants them."

"They're mine."

"I don't care if I hurt you, little girl. I do what pleases the Kingfish. He's promised to make me a true amphibian. Lung implants. A surgery he'll perform on the faithful. He told me I'll be the first. I will throw away this clumsy water-breather. I will live the glamorous amphibious lifestyle."

Archibald was silent for a moment. "Give me the glasses."

"I won't!" cried Billie.

With a heave, Archibald rolled himself over the wall of the tank. He landed on the gravel floor. He loomed over Billie. He smelled like catfood, and up close his water-breather made a hissing sound.

Archibald lunged toward her. Billie dodged to one side and hit him on the back with her fist. It bounced off as if he were made of rubber. She hit him again, and he turned his bulk around in a rage.

"Give them over," he growled, "or I'll squish you against the side of this tank till you feel like you've been flattened by a steamroller. Those shades will just pop out of your hand. Either way, they're mine."

"No they're not!" cried Billie. In one quick motion she threw the glasses onto the gravel floor and stomped them with her feet. They shattered into a million pieces.

13

The Grand Parade

"LOUDER, you furry little idiots!" Bernard Buzzard, wearing a silk top hat for the Grand Parade, looked down on the Aqualand Glee Club from his perch on a rolling float. An ostrich, the long skinny legs of her white spangled jumpsuit flapping in the breeze, led the procession. She twirled a baton in her beak and was followed by the rest of the glee club. Riding high on the float with Bernard, Billie could see something that hadn't been visible when the singers performed in the city square. They had seemed so happy there, so together. Now she could see that their cheerful smiles were strained. In the center of the group, very low to the ground, scuttled an enormous white crab. It pinched the singers with its sharp claws if any of them stopped smiling or strayed out of line. Sometimes it pinched to help one of them hit a high note.

The Aqualand Glee Club sang the same song over and over:

> *He knows about Fluff*
> *He knows about taste*
> *He's brought evolution to a whole new place!*
> *He knows about pudding*
> *He knows about songs*
> *Kingfish knows about rights and wrongs!*

They all looked as if they'd been performing nonstop since Billie saw them last. The smallest performer, the mole Billie had liked so much before, squeaked out her solo with a valiant show of forced enthusiasm. It was lucky she did. If the crab had pinched her, its claws would have crushed her tiny body in two.

> *Kingfish, I'm your biggest fan!*
> *Kingfish, I'm your biggest fan!*

Why didn't I notice this before? thought Billie. I was so caught up in admiring their cute outfits and their team spirit.

The buzzard turned to Billie. "Discipline is so important, especially for the young. This glee club gives the youth of Bixopolis a sense of belonging. Each little singer feels she's part of a group. It's an important element of a normal childhood, Billie." Bernard paused a moment, surveying the scene before them. "You should be so proud of your brother, Bix. This glorious parade is in his honor."

The float they rode on had four tiers, like a wedding cake. The buzzard rode on the bottom tier, keeping an eye on the glee club. The Kingfish's rhinoceros, a nasty-looking animal that had been completely covered with gold paint, trotted in front of the float. Billie stood on a tier she shared with Archibald. He goggled menacingly at her from inside his water-breather, keeping one wet fin on her shoulder at all times. "Don't try anything, little mammal," he grunted.

On the next tier of the wedding cake was Bix, in a steel cage full of pillows. He still wore rose-colored glasses, and occasionally dipped a pudgy hand into a vat of vanilla pudding. His clothes were dirty. He looked like a mindless little ball of fat.

On top of the wedding cake float rode the Kingfish. He wore a white spangled jacket and his huge orange fishtail wound down around the lower tiers of the float like an enormous snake. Every so often it would twitch and smack the side with a great slapping sound.

Behind the wedding cake float rode the Groupers on their motorcycles. After them was a second float, carrying a model of the Bixopolis of the future. Its centerpiece was a statue of the Kingfish, taller than the tallest skyscraper, watching over the entire city. Your Library Goat was riding next to the model. She babbled on and on, a look of resignation in her watery eyes: "The Bixopolis of tomorrow will be a city of wonders. In the name of the Kingfish, I promise you a future in which every creature will be able to mix and match species to its heart's content. You don't need to keep living your pathetic little furry life! There's more to existence than a squawk and a preening of feathers! Tell your friends out in the countryside. Come to Bixopolis! Live with the Kingfish!"

The Grand Parade marched on through the city. No one watched it. There were no cheering crowds along the streets. Once a flamingo with a bottle of Strawberry Fizz under its pink wing staggered out of a doorway and shouted, "To hell with the Kingfish!" Despite the noise of motorcycles, the singing, and Your Library Goat's endless droning, the whole event seemed somehow quiet, solemn, and strange.

They marched by a huge wall poster. It showed the Kingfish embracing Bix, his serpent's tail encircling them both. It read:

KINGFISH AND BIX

THEY KNOW WHAT'S GOOD FOR YOU!

The Grand Parade stopped in the middle of the town square Billie had visited before. A ragtag group of animals was gathered for the ceremony, most of them tough-looking pigs and flamingos. Among them stood Cairo T. Crow, holding a sign that read WELCOME, WONDERBOY! Billie's eye was drawn to a small green animal hiding between the two front legs of a particularly obese pig. The animal suddenly lifted up its cap and winked one bulging eye right at Billie. It was King Buster! Archibald's oily fin tightened on Billie's shoulder as she caught her breath in recognition. Buster disappeared into the crowd.

When the floats were all parked around the edge of the square, two Groupers carried Bix into a narrow wooden shed. There, the Wonderboy would remain hidden so he could make his big entrance after the Kingfish's speech.

Archibald grabbed Billie by the hair and yanked her forcefully down off the float. "Don't make trouble," he warned. He dragged her into the shed. Inside, it smelled of rotten herring. Bix drooled quietly in his cage. He barely noticed Billie.

"Stay here and keep that Bix baby quiet or I'll squish you into sea-slop," threatened Archibald. "You're not the Wonderboy. I don't have to treat you like a little prince." Breathing loudly through his scuba gear,

Archibald stood guard menacingly in the doorway. There was no way out of the shed.

Billie peered out through a crack in the wooden wall. Where was King Buster?

The Kingfish sat on a throne in the center of the town square. The thick coils of his tail were folded underneath him. He began to speak. "My adoring fans! My revolutionary evolutionary rule is already expanding into every corner of the Borderland. Once every creature of swamp and woodland has learned to love me, I will leave you. I will journey across the Endless Desert back to my homeland, to stagger their piddly human brains with my wisdom and my beauty.

"Who will take care of you then? Who will guide you? Who will protect you?" The Kingfish's voice rose to a wailing shout, and his tail slapped the ground with a sound like thunder. "There is someone! The one who founded the new Bixopolis! I AM THE FUTURE. HE IS THE FUTURE."

Archibald seemed hypnotized by the Kingfish. He stared at the throne. Behind Billie, a wooden panel began to wiggle. In a moment it was pulled aside, and the mustachioed face of Uncle Myron appeared in the opening! At last! Billie wanted to yelp with joy, but Uncle Myron put a finger to his lips. He reached a long arm into the shed and grabbed Billie's wrist.

"Come on!" Myron whispered. "Now's our chance!" He tugged Billie toward the opening. "Bix!" she whispered.

"BIX! THE WONDERBOY! MY SON AND HEIR!" screamed the Kingfish to the crowd.

Billie grabbed Bix through the bars of his cage. They'd be coming for him any second! He gurgled, starting to say something, but she clamped a hand over his mouth. She tried to pull him through the bars. If only he hadn't gotten so fat! She managed to yank him about halfway out, and then his pudgy belly stuck fast.

She checked on Archibald. He was still absorbed in the Kingfish's speech, but Bix was starting to whimper, so she had to be quick. Billie dipped her hand into the vat of pudding. She'd grease him up. As fast as she could, she rubbed sticky vanilla glop all over her brother's waist.

It worked! With a slushy sound, Bix slipped through the bars and into her arms. Ripping off the rose-colored glasses that were tied to his head, Billie pulled Bix quickly through the hole Uncle Myron had made in the back of the shed. There, hiding her bulk behind a parked float, kneeled Madame Zanoni. On her back was King Buster, peeking out from under a corner of his wife's pink bathrobe. Myron helped Billie and Bix climb carefully into Zanoni's enormous pocket. Scrunched down, they couldn't be seen.

"Shake it, honey," said King Buster to Zanoni. "We gotta get outta here while the fishbrain's got their attention."

Myron leaped onto Zanoni's back, and he and Buster hid under her large floppy collar. The old lady tiptoed away from the festivities in the square and turned down a dark alley where no one would see them.

Myron whispered urgently, "Madame Z., do your best. We need to put as much distance as we can between ourselves and Bixopolis."

Back in the town square, the Kingfish took a small throne out from behind his own and placed it alongside. He smoothed his sideburns, then signaled Archibald to bring Bix. He raised both arms high and proudly flicked his tail.

"MEET THE WONDERBOY! KNEEL! KNEEL!"

As the pigs and flamingos knelt down on the hard cobblestones, Archibald turned and ducked inside the shed. A moment later he reappeared, his eyes goggled out in surprise and fury. He lumbered over to where Bernard Buzzard stood with Cairo T. Crow.

"Bernie!" Archibald gurgled in a low voice. "Bernie, we got a problem."

14

End of a Tail

Madame Zanoni was getting tired. Tucked in the pocket of the bathrobe, Billie could feel the elephant's sides wheezing as she galloped out of town. Heaving and snorting, Madame slowed to a trot as soon as they reached the countryside.

"Zanoni! Keep going!" cried Myron. "They're sure to come after us!"

Madame stumbled over a rock as she tried to pick up speed. "I can't," she moaned. "I've been running for miles and miles."

"Babycakes, you better try," croaked her husband. "Listen! It's them." Sure enough, the roar of the Groupers' cycles could be heard in the distance. Holding Billie's hand in the darkness of the pocket, Bix whimpered. The sound grew louder.

"Run, Zanoni, run!" cried Myron. "They're catching up to us!"

With a burst of speed, Madame shot forward, every muscle straining. They neared the edge of the Endless Desert.

"Faster, my love! Those cycles are built for speed!" called Buster, who was keeping a lookout behind. Suddenly, the elephant's knees buckled. She lurched forward, gasping for breath. Billie and Bix were thrown forcefully out of the pocket and landed sprawling on a pile of leaves. Zanoni had collapsed entirely.

"We have to revive her!" cried Buster, hopping down to the ground. "My love! Can you stand?" Zanoni made no response except a feeble wave of her trunk.

"Kids, are you okay?" asked Myron, rushing over to them. The roar of the approaching motorcycles grew louder.

"We can't leave her here," cried Buster, fanning his wife with his hat. "The Groupers will get her! Come here and pinch her cheeks!" As Billie ran over, King Buster froze. "Wait! What's that hanging around your neck?"

The Frog was staring at Billie's medallion, a plastic circle with the word INSURANCE printed on it in purple letters. She'd forgotten it completely.

"The Clam gave you this, right?" asked Buster, fanning Zanoni again.

"Yes," answered Billie. "But—"

"Say the insurance words, quick!" ordered Buster. "The Groupers'll be here any second."

"What words?"

"How should I know what words?" King Buster shouted back. He was flapping Zanoni's right ear back and forth now to wake her up. "The Clam told you. He always does."

Billie clutched the medallion in her hand. What words? The Groupers' motorcycles topped a hill and bore down on them. What words? Billie looked helplessly at the morning sky. There was a pale crescent moon—and it came to her. It must be!

"BEST SERVICE UNDER THE MOON!" Billie shouted. She felt the medallion jump in her hand, and when she looked back down at it, the word INSURANCE was gone. CLAIMED, it read. At the same moment, out of a cloud of desert sand, the Silver Moon Motel zigged and zagged to a stop in front of them.

The Clam leaned out the office window. "Hop on! Hop on, missie!" Billie, Bix, and Buster clambered onto the rickety wooden balcony of the motel. With an immense effort, Myron pushed the groggy Madame

Zanoni up the steps. She immediately fell down again on the porch and lay there exhausted. As soon as Myron himself set foot on the bottom step, the Silver Moon Motel leaped into motion. Billie looked back toward the Groupers. They were still close, pursuing at top speed, but the motel was faster. The Groupers started to fall behind.

Quickly, Billie brought Bix into one of the motel rooms. "Stay in here, Bixie, and don't come out unless I say it's okay." Bix nodded. He had lost his vacant look. Taking off those rose-colored glasses and not having pudding for a while had certainly improved him; he was more normal already.

Billie returned to the porch, which was shaking and tilting as the motel zigzagged across the desert. The Groupers had fallen farther behind, but they were still visible in a cloud of sand. Buster was comforting Zanoni by standing on her head and whispering in her ear. Myron hung on to the railing of the porch for dear life. "Faster!" he shouted to the Clam. "Faster!"

There was a high-pitched whine, and then a sound like marbles banging around in a garbage can. The motel jerked to a stop.

"Oh, no," screamed Billie. "It's broken down again. What'll we do?"

"Don't worry," said the Clam, rolling out of the office door, followed by a gush of sand and water. It had a tool belt slung around its shell. "It's the defibrillator. I can fix it in a second." It rolled quickly down the steps and disappeared under the motel.

But it wasn't quick enough.

The Groupers pulled up alongside the motel, spraying sand as they screeched their cycles to a halt. Riding scrunched next to each other in the sidecar were Bernard Buzzard and Cairo T. Crow.

"Hatched to Ride!" Archibald burbled. "HATCHED TO RIDE!" yelled the Groupers in chorus. Their water-breather pumps made a horrible gurgly sound.

Without a word, Madame Zanoni struggled to her feet, shook herself, straightened her bathrobe with her trunk, and stepped carefully down off the porch. She bravely faced the Groupers, standing between them and the motel. Uncle Myron, with King Buster on his shoulder, came forward and stood beside her. Billie stayed, guarding the motel door which hid her brother.

The buzzard and the crow fluttered into the air and landed in front of the elephant. The Groupers rolled forward behind them, their fins curled into tight fists. Bernard brushed the dust of the road off himself with one gray wing.

"Madame Zanoni," he said, "I'm sorry a balletomane like myself could not meet you in happier circumstances. I'm a great admirer of your *Dying Swan*."

"Don't flatter me, you lying fraud," snapped Madame Zanoni.

"Have it your way, you talentless old fatso." Bernard eyed Billie, standing on the motel porch. "*Enchanté*, Billie my dear."

"Hey, Myron!" Cairo squawked. "My old card buddy! How you doing? Hey, I'm crying for you, I really am. When I see a fellow being about to get squished, all 'cause he won't let a little tyke have his pudding, I get all weepy inside."

The crow took a bottle of Strawberry Fizz out from under one wing and drained it. He peered under the motel. "Come outta there, Shellshock. We don't want the Silver Moon zigzagging away on us." The Clam rolled out from under the motel, still holding a screwdriver.

"And that's all of you, I think," oozed the buzzard. "Except for one. Bring out Bix. The Kingfish wants him."

"Yeah. He wants him now," burbled Luther.

"Bring him out or we'll squish you. All of you, beginning with that tone-deaf, talentless frog musician. Buster," said Archibald with a sneer, "squishing you would be a pleasure and a service to the music-loving public."

"Don't listen to them, dearie." Madame Zanoni soothed her husband in her quiet voice. "You're the best I ever worked with and the love of my life."

"Or maybe we should begin with the wrinkled bag of blubber," threatened Archibald. "We'll squish her trunk so hard she can't breathe."

"Make way for your Kingfish!" cried a deep, mournful voice. The gilded rhinoceros from the parade was approaching the Silver Moon Motel. It was followed by a curious crowd of pigs, flamingos, and other animals. The members of the Aqualand Glee Club trailed tiredly behind. On the rhino's golden back rode the Kingfish, his tail coiled around himself.

Nobody moved. A quiet moaning began. The Kingfish slithered down to the ground, his huge tail twitching and uncoiling behind him. His strange body heaved with sobs. Billie couldn't believe it. He was crying.

"Bixie! Please, my Wonderboy! Come back to your Kingfish! You can have anything you want. Anything." The Kingfish was still sobbing, his whole body trembling. "You still love me, Bix! I know you do! Come out!" The Kingfish's voice took on an insistent, hypnotic tone. "I am the future. You are the future. I am your Kingfish. You are my son."

No Bix. He was safe in the motel room.

The Kingfish ground his teeth in fury. He reared up to his full scaly height, twenty feet in the air on his sea serpent's tail. "BIX! NO MORE PUDDING!" he screamed. "I'll throw your sister down a well! I'll beat you till you're black and blue. BIX! COME HERE AND LOVE ME!"

Again the Kingfish sobbed, and this time his voice broke. "I know you're in there, Bixie. I've told the world you're my son and heir. Please. Billie? Give back my Bix."

"NO WAY!" yelled Billie. "He's never going back to you, you pudding pervert!"

The Kingfish screamed back at her: "If Bix isn't out here in one minute, my Groupers start squishing!" The huge fish stood by their motorcycles, waiting for the signal to smother everyone with their slippery bodies.

As Billie watched them in terror, desperately trying to think of a way out, she had the strangest sensation. She thought she heard, from a great distance, Billie Holiday singing "Cheap Carnations." She looked up. Sailing through the sky was Uncle Myron's fishtail Cadillac convertible, with a human who could only be Mommie Darling at the wheel. Billie could see Clark Kent—repaired, and with a new watermelon head—in the seat alongside Mommie. The Groupers looked up. Even the Kingfish looked up.

The Caddy dove down, swooping over the line of Groupers. Clark's voice boomed out over speakers: "Kent here. Live from the Silver Moon Motel. ACTION! ACTION! ACTION!" A metal door opened on the underside of the Cadillac. From it, a hose showered white gluey glop down on the Groupers, coating their water-breathers.

"Have some marshmallow soup!" cried Mommie. She had sacrificed her favorite food, the last of the case Myron had brought her.

The Groupers were totally covered, goop dripping down their breather helmets. They waddled about on their tail fins, blinded and confused. There was nothing they could do. They couldn't take off their water-breathers or they'd die. In their panic, they crashed into one another and flopped helplessly on the ground.

"Come back here, you idiot fishes! Bring me my Bix!" screamed the Kingfish. "Squish them! Squish them all!"

Billie had been watching from the motel porch. Suddenly, from behind her, she heard Bix cry out her name. "Billixa! GROUPUS!" She rushed into the motel room where she'd been keeping Bix hidden. The back wall had been smashed through! Archibald, dripping with marshmallow glop, held a screaming Bix under one oily fin.

"Stop! Let him go!" Billie yelled.

"Go away, little girl," growled Archibald. "The boy's mine, my passport to the amphibious lifestyle!" He turned his back to Billie and moved toward the jagged opening in the wall. Billie launched herself at the huge fish. She leaped high and grabbed his water-breather helmet with both hands. She held on tight and banged with all her strength on the heavy glass dome. Archibald dropped Bix, clawing at Billie with both fins, trying to tear her off. Billie ripped at the rubber seal that kept the water in the closed dome. It wouldn't budge. Archibald waddled to a wall and crushed Billie against it. He squished her harder and harder. Her ribs aching, Billie banged again with all her might on the glass of the helmet—and it cracked. Water began to trickle out. Billie pounded again and again. The trickle became a stream. Archibald panicked. He stumbled through the open door of the motel room, with Billie still clinging to his back, the water from his breather running down his scaly sides. The breather broke apart in a shower of glass. Archibald collapsed onto the ground, wheezing and choking. Then he lay still.

Billie stood up. She was soaked and her hands were

sore. Bix ran over and put his arms around her waist. He held on tight.

On the sand in front of the motel, two other Groupers lay motionless. They had flopped over in sticky confusion and Madame Zanoni had cracked both their water-breather helmets with one well-placed blow of her foot. The remaining marshmallow-covered Groupers staggered back to their motorcycles. They roared off blindly, swerving as they went. Luther screamed, "Spawned to Be Wild!" and promptly smashed into a nearby tree. His motorcycle burst into flames.

The gilded rhinoceros had run off as well, but could still be seen in the distance, sniffing at some hole in the desert sand. The animals from the Aqualand Glee Club had thrown their uniforms on the ground. Along with a few pigs and flamingos, they were dancing for joy, skipping and singing:

> *No more Groupers*
> *No more fish*
> *We'll have pudding*
> *With every dish*

Bernard Buzzard, realizing he was on the losing side, spread his molting gray wings and flew rapidly away.

Cairo T. Crow hopped over to Uncle Myron, Billie, and Bix. "Myron," he squawked. "This little incident isn't going to damage our relationship, is it? We can still play Old Maid at the Silver Moon?"

"Get out of here, Cairo," bellowed Uncle Myron. "I can't believe I ever let you deal. I never want to see you again."

"Me neither," said Billie. "You're a liar and a cheater and you drink too much Fizz."

"That's what my ex-wife used to say," croaked Cairo, and launched himself into the air. In a moment, he was just a speck in the sky.

The Kingfish was alone. He had no one left to order around, and no three-hundred-pound fish to do his dirty work. He was weeping pitifully, curled up in his tail. "Bixie, how could you do this to me?" he was moaning, his face in his hands. "After all that pudding I gave you?"

Billie held Bix's hand tight, but it didn't look like he wanted to go to the Kingfish, anyway. Without those rose-colored glasses, he wanted to be with his sister.

Mommie Darling landed the Cadillac and stepped out, with Clark Kent right behind her. Gone was the nightgown she had worn for the past ten years. She was dressed in striped mechanic's overalls and platform shoes. "Look me over, you handsome walrus," she said to Myron. "I'm back in circulation. As soon as Clark got home, bent and battered from risking his circuits to help someone else, I realized it wasn't him who needed reprogramming. It was me. I decided I better get out of bed and give you and Billie a hand. Besides, it was about time I rejoined the rest of the world.

"By the way, I have to confess," she said, batting her eyelashes at Myron. "I've been hiding your Cadillac so you wouldn't leave the Borderland. Fixit found it in Bogbottom Swamp days ago. All it needed was a paint job.

"Now," she said briskly, "let's have a look at the man who never had enough manners to come and greet me when he arrived in the Borderland." Mommie marched over to the Kingfish, who had been hiding his face in his hands with occasional pleading glances in Bix's direction. Something about him stopped Mommie in her tracks. "It can't be!" she said to herself, and took a step closer. She peered into his face.

"You?" Mommie said as soon as he looked up. "It's you, you little weasel!"

"Shirley," said the Kingfish. "I didn't mean to—"

"You conniving thief of love!" cried Mommie. "Ladies and gentlemen, meet Herman Mudhen, my ex-husband and the slimiest man ever born. He left me at Caesar's Palace in Las Vegas, Nevada, on our honeymoon. Walked out with a showgirl and never came back."

Mommie Darling picked up a loop of the Kingfish's powerful tail. "Look at this thing! Mudhen, did you have the creatures in the city believing this tail?"

The animals began to crowd in closer, peering nervously at their former leader.

"I only wanted them to think I was important. Shirley, I still love you. I only wanted to—"

"Shut up, Herman!" said Mommie Darling. She took a knife out of her pocket and slit the Kingfish's tail open. The scaly orange skin peeled back, exposing a mass of springs, wires, and gears. Mommie reached inside, tugged on a lever, and the entire tail came loose from the Kingfish and flopped onto the ground. The animals gasped.

The Kingfish stood there, a small human in his underwear, with skinny white legs. Mommie Darling turned to her audience. "He learned a few electromechanical tricks from me during our engagement. The tail's not bad work." She turned back to the Kingfish. "Mudhen, you haven't changed. You're still a weasel, through and through."

Uncle Myron stepped forward. "There's no place for a Kingfish in the Borderland. Good-bye, Mudhen."

The Kingfish had no choice. He walked slowly over to Archibald's motorcycle and hauled it upright. He swung himself onto the seat.

"Good-bye, all of you," he said. "Don't think you've seen the last of me." He started the engine. "Good-bye, Bix. We might have done great things."

The Kingfish roared off into the wide and empty Endless Desert.

15

Encore

Mommie Darling threw her arms around Uncle Myron and kissed him on the lips.

Gross, thought Billie. Right on his walrus mustache.

"Kissy floopus!" shouted Bix.

"Get in the car, kids," growled Myron.

Billie and Bix piled into the front seat of the fishtail Cadillac. Mommie had repainted it—the same old lovely sky blue. Myron started the engine with a roar and they soared up, smooth and steady, high into the air. Looking down, Billie waved. Clark was looking up at her, and he swiveled his camera back and forth to say good-bye.

"All those creatures will make themselves sick on pudding and marshmallows," said Uncle Myron, turning the wheel as the Caddy tilted into a steeper climb. "They've been deprived so long, they won't be able to restrain themselves." The figures in the landscape below dwindled and disappeared. Myron chuckled to himself and steadied the car at a smooth cruising altitude.

"Pudding never makes *me* sick." It was Bix talking.

"Maybe not, but it's still not good for you—" Billie stopped short, realizing what she'd just heard. Bix's first real sentence! Maybe the Kingfish's suffocating smother-love had made him eager to grow up a little.

"Congrats, Bixie," said Billie, squeezing his cheek. "You spoke! In English!"

She looked down. The landscape was a sandy tan as far as she could see in every direction. The Endless Desert. Then Myron drove into a cloud. It was cool and damp and so thick Billie could barely see her uncle in the driver's seat. She grabbed Bix's hand. They sailed through the cloud for the longest time in a hushed silence, listening only to the dim purr of the motor.

"Uncle Myron?" Billie asked, squinting through the mist.

"Yes?"

"How did you first get over there? Was it an accident or something?"

"Get over where?" Myron asked, raising an eyebrow. They burst out of the cloud and the Cadillac began to tilt downward.

"The Borderland," Billie answered. She was sure he already knew what she meant.

"The Borderland, eh? Must be somewhere beyond the clouds. Serious people like you and me don't believe in that kind of thing. And if someone did, like little Bixie here, no one would listen to him, anyway. Take the advice of your wise old Uncle Myron, Billie: Learn to keep a secret." He switched on the tape player. Billie Holiday's smoky voice wailed loudly into the air.

> *Don't give me no carnations, baby.*
> *I'm a roses kind of girl. . . .*

Billie was thoughtful. "What'll Brian and Mimi say?" she persisted. "Where do they think I've been?"

"With me. You left in my car. You're coming back in my car." Myron chuckled at his own cleverness.

"Is that what you told them?"

"Well, I didn't tell them personally," answered Myron, "since I've been someplace else we won't mention. But I do have certain ways of getting messages across. I let your parents know you were safe with me."

Billie knew Uncle Myron was right. Who would believe her, anyway? Besides, Mimi and Brian had been saved an awful lot of worry.

Myron pointed over the side. "Look, kids! We're almost home." Billie peered eagerly down. She didn't recognize the landscape below. This was not Omaha.

There were no flat plains, no downtown with tall hotels. This wasn't New York either, where Brian and Mimi had a penthouse. No bustling city streets, no Twin Towers, no yellow taxis honking their horns. Instead, she saw smooth green lawns with flower beds and big houses with picture windows set far back from the street.

"Where are we?" she asked.

"Upstate New York," answered Uncle Myron. "A nice little town with a pretty good school. Look! There's the baseball field!" Billie could see the sandy diamond. Some kids were practicing in the outfield. The Caddy flew low and lower, finally touching down with a slight bump on an empty road lined with trees. They cruised along for a minute, then turned up a long dirt driveway. At the top of a low hill, a big comfortable house came into view. A dark-eyed raccoon darted under a bush as the car came to a stop by the front door.

"Myron! Kids!" It was Mimi, coming around from the back of the house in a silver dress and a big straw hat. She looked beautiful. Brian was right behind her, holding his guitar in one hand. Billie and Bix leaped out of the car and ran to them.

Mimi showered them with lipsticky kisses and Brian danced around strumming his guitar in cheerful chords. Bix jumped up and down on his pudgy legs. "Mimi! Brian!" he shouted, pronouncing his parents' names for the first time. Mimi and Brian were thrilled.

Myron leaned back against the hood of the Caddy, basking in the sunlight. Billie looked over at him as she wiped Mimi's lipstick off her face. He looked back at her and winked.

A few moments later, Uncle Myron started up the car. "I've got very important things to do," he bellowed, waving good-bye and rolling the Caddy backward down the long driveway. "Very important indeed! Bye-bye, Billie! Bye-bye, Bix!"

"Come back soon!" they all called. The blue convertible turned the corner and Myron was gone.

Mimi, holding Billie by the hand, gave her the grand tour of their new house. It was made of that gray weathered wood you see in New England houses, and was much bigger than their apartment in New York. There was a sunny, open kitchen with yellow curtains, and Billie's room had a canopy bed. There was a pink and black bicycle for Billie in the garage, and a trike for Bix. There was a wide grassy front yard, and in the backyard, a swimming pool.

All four of them took off their shoes and dangled their feet in the water. Mimi explained, "We just canceled the rest of the tour, baby."

"The publicist had a fit," added Brian, "and our accountant had two fits."

"Screamed themselves silly," continued Mimi. "What about the road crew? The record company? What about the fans? What about the *money*?" Brian laughed and strummed a few dramatic chords on the guitar. "We didn't care about all that," Mimi went on. "As soon as you ran away, all we wanted was to have you home again."

"The hype of the concert tour had taken over our lives," Brian added. He picked up Bix and bounced him on his knee. Bixie shrieked and giggled. "We were giving more to our fans than we were to our kids. Now it's time for the slow lane, for a while anyway. The road can wait."

"We just wanted to find you," said Mimi, "and make a real home for all of us. Do you like it, Billie?"

Billie looked around. It looked just like the family houses she'd read about in books. "Yeah," she said, splashing her feet in the water. "When I get used to it, I think I will." She didn't say what she really felt, which was that it seemed like someone else's home, not Mimi and Brian's. What happened to all Brian's recording equipment? His roomful of musical instruments? Where were Mimi's feather boas? The house seemed empty, not just of stuff, but also of people. When they were on the road, there were always backup singers floating around the hotel suite drinking hot lemon tea for their throats, or loud record producers dropping names and calling everyone "darling." The phone was always ringing off the hook, and Mimi's personal trainer, Roberta, was usually lifting weights in the hallway. Half-opened suitcases overflowed with sparkly performance clothes, reporters would scuttle in anxiously, carrying tape recorders. Mimi's room was always filled with flowers.

This big country house was beautiful. It was organized. It was incredibly normal. But it wasn't home.

Billie didn't say any of this. Instead she asked, "Where's the Pigbone?"

"He went to the Bahamas on vacation and never came back." Brian laughed.

"He fell madly in love," explained Mimi, "under an island moon. He sent us a postcard about it."

"No great loss, Billie," said Brian.

"We thought you'd go to school in the fall, honey," Mimi said to Billie, "with all the other kids. And I signed you up for baseball. They have a team that starts practice next month for summer Little League."

Billie smiled. Baseball was something she really wanted to do. "That's great, Mimi."

"Maybe Roberta can help you get back into it," her

mother suggested. "I think she was a pitcher when she was a kid."

"Roberta?" Maybe their old life hadn't totally disappeared. "Is she still around?"

"Are you joking, baby?" Mimi laughed. "I could never survive without Roberta. I've got a shoot for the cover of *Vanity Fair* in two weeks! She's getting me in shape. She moves in tomorrow, with a half dozen exercise machines."

"She does?"

"Of course!"

"And you're gonna be on the cover?"

Mimi put her arms around Billie. "What did you think? I'd sit around and bake cookies all day just 'cause you're going to school? We're only an hour from New York City, baby! Life ain't over 'cause we've got a house in the country."

"We've got the movers coming on Thursday with the recording equipment," added Brian. "We're building a studio in the basement where we can set up. Totally soundproof."

"Brian's been writing some new music," said Mimi.

"One song so far," he explained. "I wrote it after you ran away. It's about you and Bixie. We're thinking it might be the title track of a new album."

A song about her! The start of a new album! Billie

was glad her parents were still making music; glad they hadn't given up their crazy rock-and-roll lives; and glad, too, to have a baseball team to play on and a school to go to in the fall.

Late that night, after Mimi had tucked her in with a kiss and departed, leaving a trail of perfume in the warm night air, Billie stared up at the silken canopy of her new bed. Downstairs, she could hear Brian fooling around on the grand piano. Mimi's crystal voice sang low, making up snatches of lyric. Billie smiled to herself as she drifted into her dreams. She was home.